# AGATHA RAISIN
# AND THE
# CASE OF THE
# CURIOUS CURATE

# PREVIOUS MYSTERIES BY M. C. BEATON

*The Skeleton in the Closet*

## Agatha Raisin

*Agatha Raisin and the Day the Floods Came*
*Agatha Raisin and the Love from Hell*
*Agatha Raisin and the Fairies of Fryfam*
*Agatha Raisin and the Witch of Wyckhadden*
*Agatha Raisin and the Wizard of Evesham*
*Agatha Raisin and the Wellspring of Death*
*Agatha Raisin and the Terrible Tourist*
*Agatha Raisin and the Murderous Marriage*
*Agatha Raisin and the Walkers of Dembley*
*Agatha Raisin and the Potted Gardener*
*Agatha Raisin and the Vicious Vet*
*Agatha Raisin and the Quiche of Death*

## Hamish Macbeth

*Death of an Addict*
*Death of a Scriptwriter*
*Death of a Dentist*
*Death of a Macho Man*
*Death of a Nag*
*Death of a Charming Man*
*Death of a Travelling Man*
*Death of a Glutton*
*Death of a Prankster*
*Death of a Snob*
*Death of a Hussy*
*Death of a Perfect Wife*
*Death of an Outsider*
*Death of a Cad*
*Death of a Gossip*

# AGATHA RAISIN AND THE CASE OF THE CURIOUS CURATE

†

## M. C. BEATON

ST. MARTIN'S MINOTAUR
NEW YORK

Bea

www.minotaurbooks.com

Library of Congress Cataloging-in-Publication Data

Beaton, M. C.
    Agatha Raisin and the case of the curious curate / M.C. Beaton.—1st ed.
        p. cm.
    ISBN 0-312-20768-9
    1. Raisin, Agatha (Fictitious character)—Fiction.    2. Women detectives—England—Cotswold Hills—Fiction.    3. Cotswold Hills (England)—Fiction.
4. Clergy—Crimes against—Fiction.    5. Divorced women—Fiction.
I. Title.

PR6052.E196 A64 2003
823'.914—dc21

                                                          2002031885

First Edition: March 2003

10   9   8   7   6   5   4   3   2   1

This book is dedicated to Mrs. Nancy Stubbs of Woore, near Crewe, with many thanks for her description of the village duck races, which were much more decorous than the one described in this book.

# AGATHA RAISIN
## AND THE
## CASE OF THE
## CURIOUS CURATE

# ONE

✝

AGATHA Raisin was beginning to feel that nothing would ever interest her again. She had written to a monastery in France, to her ex-husband, James Lacey, who, she believed, was taking holy orders, only to receive a letter a month later saying that they had not heard from Mr. Lacey. Yes, he had left and promised to return, but they had heard or seen nothing of him.

So, she thought miserably, James had simply been sick of her and had wanted a divorce and had used the monastery as a way to get out of the marriage. She swore she would never be interested in a man again, and that included her neighbour, John Armitage. He had propositioned her and had been turned down. Agatha had been hurt because he had professed no admiration or love for her. They talked from time to time when they met in the village, but Agatha refused all invitations to dinner and so he had finally given up asking her.

So the news that the vicar, Alf Bloxby, was to get a curate buzzed around the village, but left Agatha unmoved. She went regularly to church because of her friendship with the vicar's wife, regarding it more as a duty that anything to do with spiritual uplift. Also because of her friendship with Mrs. Bloxby, she felt compelled to attend the Carsely Ladies' Society where the village women discussed their latest fund-raising projects.

It was a warm August evening when Agatha trotted wearily along to the vicarage. She looked a changed Agatha. No make-up, sensible flat sandals and a loose cotton dress.

Miss Simms, the secretary, read the minutes of the last meeting. They were all out in the vicarage garden. Agatha barely listened, watching instead how Miss Simms's stiletto heels sank lower and lower into the grass.

Mrs. Bloxby had recently been elected chairwoman. Definitely the title of chairwoman. No chairpersons in Carsely. After tea and cakes had been passed round, she addressed the group. "As you know, ladies, our new curate will be arriving next week. His name is Tristan Delon and I am sure we all want to give him a warm welcome. We shall have a reception here on the following Wednesday. Everyone in the village of Carsely has been invited."

"Won't that be rather a crush?" asked Miss Jellop, a thin, middle-aged lady with a lisping voice and large protruding eyes. Agatha thought unkindly that she looked like a rabbit with myxomatosis.

"I don't think there will be all that much interest," said Mrs. Bloxby ruefully. "I am afraid church attendances are not very high these days."

Agatha thought cynically that the lure of free food and

drinks would bring them in hordes. She wondered whether to say anything, and then a great weariness assailed her. It didn't matter. She herself would not be going. She had recently returned from London, where she had taken on a free-lance public relations job for the launch of a new soap called Mystic Health, supposed to be made from Chinese herbs. Agatha had balked at the name, saying that people didn't want healthy soap, they wanted pampering soap, but the makers were adamant. She was about to go back to London for the launch party and intended to stay for a week and do some shopping.

At the end of the following week, Agatha made her way to Paddington Station, wondering, as she had wondered before, why London did not hold any magic for her anymore. It seemed dusty and dingy, noisy and threatening. She had not particularly enjoyed the launch of the new soap, feeling she was moving in a world to which she no longer belonged. But what was waiting for her in her home village of Carsely? Nothing. Nothing but domestic chores, the ladies' society, and pottering about the village.

But when she collected her car at Moreton-in-Marsh Station and began the short drive home, she felt a lightening of her spirits. She would call on Mrs. Bloxby and sit in the cool green of the vicarage garden and feel soothed.

Mrs. Bloxby was pleased to see her. "Come in, Mrs. Raisin," she said. Although she and Agatha had been friends for some time, they still used the formal "Mrs." when addressing each other, a tradition of the ladies' society, which fought a rearguard action against modern times and modern manners. "Isn't it hot?" exclaimed the vicar's wife, pushing a damp tendril of grey hair away from her face. "We'll sit in the garden. What is your news?"

Over the teacups Agatha regaled her with a highly embroidered account of her experiences in London. "And how's the new curate?" she finally asked.

"Getting along splendidly. Poor Alf is laid low with a summer cold and Mr. Delon has been taking the services." She giggled. "I haven't told Alf, but last Sunday there was standing room only in the church. Women had come from far and wide."

"Why? Is he such a good preacher?"

"It's not that. More tea? Help yourself to milk and sugar. No, I think it is because he is so very beautiful."

"Beautiful? A beautiful curate? Is he gay?"

"Now why should you assume that a beautiful young man must be gay?"

"Because they usually are," said Agatha gloomily.

"No, I don't think he's gay. He is very charming. You should come to church this Sunday and see for yourself."

"I might do that. Nothing else to do here."

"I hate it when you get bored," said the vicar's wife anxiously. "It seems to me that every time you get bored, a murder happens somewhere."

"Murder happens every day all over the place."

"I meant close by."

"I'm not interested in murders. That last case I nearly got myself killed. I had a letter from that Detective Inspector Brudge in Worcester just before I left. He suggested I should go legit and set up my own detective agency."

"Now that's a good idea."

"I would spend my days investigating nasty divorces or working undercover in firms to find out which typist has been nicking the office stationery. No, it's not for me. Is this curate living with you?"

"We found him a room in the village with old Mrs. Feathers. As you know, she lives opposite the church, so we were lucky. Of course, we were prepared to house him here, we have plenty of room, but he would not hear of it. He says he is quite comfortably off. He has a small income from a family trust."

"I'd better get back to my cats," said Agatha, rising. "I think they prefer Doris Simpson to me." Mrs. Simpson was Agatha's cleaner, who looked after the cats when Agatha was away.

"So you will come to church on Sunday?" asked Mrs. Bloxby. "I am curious to learn what you make of our curate."

"Why, I wonder," said Agatha, her bearlike eyes sharpening with interest. "You have reservations about him?"

"I feel he's too good to be true. I shouldn't carp. We are very lucky to have him. Truth to tell, I think my poor Alf is a little jealous. Though I said nothing about it, he heard from the parishioners about the crowds in the church."

"Must be awful to be a vicar and to be expected to act like a saint," said Agatha. "All right. I'll be there on Sunday."

When she got back to her cottage, Agatha opened all the windows and the kitchen door as well and let her cats, Hodge and Boswell, out into the garden. I don't think they even missed me, thought Agatha, watching them roll on the warm grass. Doris comes in and feeds them and lets them in and out and they are perfectly happy with her. There was a ring at the doorbell and she went to answer it. John Armitage, her neighbour, stood there.

"I just came to welcome you back," he said.

"Thanks," retorted Agatha. "Oh, well, you may as well come in and have a drink."

She was always surprised, every time she saw him, at how good-looking he was with his lightly tanned face, fair hair and green eyes. Although he was about the same age as she was herself, his face was smooth and he looked younger, a fact that annoyed her almost as much as the fact that he had propositioned her because he had thought she would be an easy lay. He was a successful detective story writer.

They carried their drinks out into the garden. "The chairs are a bit dusty," said Agatha. "Everything in the garden's dusty. So what's been going on?"

"Writing and walking. Oh, and tired to death of all the women in the village babbling about how wonderful the new curate is."

"And is he wonderful?"

"Smarmy bastard."

"You're just cross because you're no longer flavour of the month."

"Could be. Haven't you seen him?"

"I haven't had time. I'm going to church on Sunday to have a look."

"Let me know what you think. There's something wrong there."

"Like what?"

"Can't put my finger on it. He doesn't seem quite real."

"Neither do you," commented Agatha rudely.

"In what way?"

"You're . . . what? Fifty-three? And yet your skin is smooth and tanned and there's something robotic about you."

"I did apologize for having made a pass at you. You haven't forgiven me, obviously."

"Yes, I have," said Agatha quickly, although she had not. "It's just . . . you never betray any emotions. You don't have much small talk."

"I can't think of anything smaller than speculation about a new village vicar. Have you ever tried just accepting people as they are instead of as something you want them to be?"

"You mean what I see is what I get?"

"Exactly."

What Agatha really wanted was a substitute for her ex-husband and was often irritated that there was nothing romantic about John, but as she hardly ever thought things through, she crossly dismissed him as a bore.

"So is it possible we could be friends?" asked John. "I mean, I only made that one gaffe."

"Yes, all right," said Agatha. She was about to add ungraciously that she had plenty of friends, but remembered in time that before she had moved to the Cotswolds from London, she hadn't had any friends at all.

"In that case, have lunch with me after church on Sunday."

"Right," said Agatha. "Thanks."

She and John arrived at the church on Sunday exactly five minutes before the service was due to begin and found there were no seats left in the pews and they had to stand at the back.

The tenor bell in the steeple above their heads fell silent. There was a rustle of anticipation in the church. Then Tristan Delon walked up to the altar and turned around. Agatha peered round the large hat of the woman in front of her and let out a gasp of amazement.

The curate *was* beautiful. He stood there, at the altar, with a shaft of sunlight lighting up the gold curls of his hair, his pale white skin, his large blue eyes, and his perfect mouth. Agatha stood there in a daze. Mechanically, she sang the opening hymn and listened to the readings from the Bible. Then the curate mounted the pulpit and began a sermon about loving thy neighbour. He had a well-modulated voice. Agatha listened to every word of a sermon she would normally have damned as mawkish and boring.

At the end of the service, it took ages to get out of the church. So many wanted to chat to the curate, now stationed on the porch. At last, it was Agatha's turn. Tristan gazed into her eyes and held her hand firmly.

"Beautiful sermon," gushed Agatha.

He smiled warmly at her. "I am glad you could come to church," he said. "Do you live far away or are you from the village?"

"I live here. In Lilac Lane," gabbled Agatha. "Last cottage."

John coughed impatiently behind her and Agatha reluctantly moved on.

"Isn't he incredible?" exclaimed Agatha as they walked to the local pub, the Red Lion, where they had agreed earlier to have lunch.

"Humph," was John's only reply.

So when they were seated in the pub over lunch, Agatha went on, "I don't think I have ever seen such a beautiful man. And he's tall, too! About six feet, would you say?"

"There's something not quite right about him," said John. "It wasn't a sparkling sermon, either."

"Oh, you're just jealous."

"Believe it or not, Agatha, I am not in the slightest jealous. I would have thought that you, of all people, would not fall for a young man simply because of his looks like all those other silly women."

"Oh, let's talk about something else," said Agatha sulkily. "How's the new book going?"

John began to talk and Agatha let his words drift in and out of her brain while she plotted about ways and means to see the curate alone. Could she ask for spiritual guidance? No, he might tell Mrs. Bloxby and Mrs. Bloxby would see through that ruse. Maybe dinner? But she was sure he would be entertained and fêted by every woman in not only Carsely, but in the villages around.

"Don't you think so?" she realized John was asking.

"Think what?"

"Agatha, you haven't been listening to a word I've said. I think I'll write a book and call it *Death of a Curate*."

"I've got a headache," lied Agatha. "That's why I wasn't concentrating on what you were saying."

After lunch, Agatha was glad to get rid of John so that she could wrap herself in brightly coloured dreams of the curate. She longed to call on Mrs. Bloxby, but Sundays were busy days for the vicar's wife and so she had to bide her time with impatience until Monday morning. She hurried along to the vicarage, but only Alf, the vicar, was there and he told her curtly that his wife was out on her rounds.

"I went to church on Sunday," said Agatha. "I've never seen such a large congregation."

"Oh, really," he said coldly. "Let's hope it is still large when I resume my duties next Sunday. Now if you will excuse me . . ."

He gently closed the door.

Agatha stood there seething with frustration. Across the road from the church stood the house where Tristan had a room. But she could not possibly call on him. She had no excuse.

She was just walking away when she saw Mrs. Bloxby coming towards her. Agatha hailed her with delight. "Want to see me?" asked Mrs. Bloxby. "Come inside and I'll put the kettle on."

Mrs. Bloxby opened the vicarage door. The vicar's voice sounded from his study with dreadful clarity. "Is that you, dear? That awful woman's just called."

"Excuse me," said Mrs. Bloxby and darted into the study and shut the door behind her.

She emerged a few moments later, rather pink in the face.

"Poor Alf, some gypsy woman's been round pestering him to buy white heather. He's rather tetchy with the heat. I'll make tea."

"Coffee, please." Agatha followed her into the kitchen.

"We'll go into the garden and you can have a cigarette."

"You forget. I've given up smoking. That trip to the hypnotist worked. Cigarettes still taste like burning rubber, the way he said they would."

Mrs. Bloxby made coffee, put two mugs of it on a tray and carried the tray out into the garden. "This dreadful heat," she said, putting the tray down on the garden table. "It does make everyone so crotchety."

"I was at church on Sunday," began Agatha.

"So many people. Did you enjoy it?"

"Very much. Very impressed with the curate."

"Ah, our Mr. Delon. Did you see anything past his extraordinary good looks?"

"I spoke to him on the porch. He seems charming."

"He's all of that."

"You don't like him, and I know why," said Agatha.

"Why?"

"Because he is filling up the church the way Mr. Bloxby never could."

"Mrs. Raisin, when have I ever been *petty*?"

"Sorry, but he does seem such a wonderful preacher."

"Indeed! I forget what the sermon was about. Refresh my memory."

But try as she could, Agatha could not remember what it had all been about and she reddened under Mrs. Bloxby's mild gaze.

"You know, Mrs. Raisin, beauty is such a dangerous thing. It can slow character formation because people are always willing to credit the beautiful with character attributes they do not have."

"You really don't like him!"

"I do not know him or understand him. Let's leave it at that."

Agatha felt restless and discontented when she returned home. She had started to make up her face again and wear her most elegant clothes. Surely her meetings with the curate were not going to be confined to one-minute talks on a Sunday on the church porch.

The doorbell rang. Ever hopeful, Agatha checked her hair and make-up in the hall mirror before opening the door. Miss Simms, the secretary of the ladies' society, stood there.

"Come in," urged Agatha, glad of any diversion.

Miss Simms teetered after Agatha on her high heels. Because of the heat of the day, she was wearing the minimum: tube top, tiny skirt and no tights. Agatha envied women who were able to go around in hot weather without stockings or tights. When she went barelegged, her shoes rubbed her heels and the top of her feet and raised blisters.

"Isn't he gorgeous," gasped Miss Simms, flopping down on a kitchen chair. "I saw you in church."

"The curate? Yes, he's quite something to look at."

"He's more than that," breathed Miss Simms. "He's got the gift."

"What gift? Speaking in tongues?"

"Nah! Healing. I had this terrible pain in me back and I met him in the village and told him about it. He took me back to his place and he laid his hands on my back and I could feel a surge of heat."

I'll bet you could, thought Agatha, sour with jealousy.

"And the pain had gone, just like that!"

There was a clatter as Agatha's cleaner, Doris Simpson, came down the stairs carrying the vacuum cleaner. "Just going to do the sitting room and then I'll be off," she said, putting her head round the kitchen door.

"We was just talking about the new curate," said Miss Simms.

"Oh, him," snorted Doris. "Slimy bastard."

"Come back here," shouted Agatha as Doris retreated.

"What?" Doris stood in the doorway, her arms folded over her apron, Agatha's cats purring and winding their way around her legs.

"Why did you call Tristan a slimy bastard?" asked Agatha.

"I dunno." Doris scratched her grey hair. "There's something about him that gives me the creeps."

"But you don't know him, surely," complained Agatha.

"No, just an impression. Now I must get on."

"What does *she* know about anything?" grumbled Miss Simms. "She's only a cleaner," she added, forgetting that she herself was sometimes reduced to cleaning houses when she was between what she euphemistically called "gentlemen friends."

"Exactly," agreed Agatha. "What's his place like?"

"Well, Mrs. Feathers's cottage is ever so dark, but he's brightened up the room with pictures and throw rugs and that. He doesn't have his own kitchen, but old Mrs. Feathers, she cooks for him."

"Lucky Mrs. Feathers," said Agatha.

"I was wondering if there was any chance of a date."

Agatha stiffened. "He's a man of the cloth," she said severely.

"But he ain't Catholic. He can go out with girls same as anybody."

"What about your gentleman friend in bathroom fittings?"

Miss Simms giggled. "He wouldn't have to know. Anyway, he's married."

The normally pushy Agatha was beginning to feel out classed. Besides, Tristan was young—well, maybe thirty-something, and Miss Simms was in her late twenties.

When Miss Simms had left, Agatha nervously paced up and down. She jerked open a kitchen drawer and found herself looking down at a packet of cigarettes. She took it out, opened it and lit one. Glory be! It tasted marvellous. The hypnotist's curse had gone. She hung on to the kitchen table until the first wave of dizziness had passed. Think what you're doing to your health, your lungs, screamed the governess in her head. "Shove off," muttered Agatha to the inner voice.

There was another ring at the doorbell. Probably some other woman come to gloat about a laying-on of hands by the curate, thought Agatha sourly.

She jerked open the door.

Tristan stood there, smiling at her.

Agatha blinked at the vision in blue shirt and blue chinos. "Oh, Mr. Delon," she said weakly. "How nice."

"Call me Tristan," he said. "I noticed you at church on Sunday. And I heard that you used to live in London. I'm still a city boy and still out of my depth in the country. This is very last minute, but I wondered whether you would be free to have dinner with me tonight?"

"Yes, that would be lovely," said Agatha, wishing she had put on a thicker layer of make-up. "Where?"

"Oh, just at my place, if that's all right."

"Lovely. What time?"

"Eight o'clock."

"Fine. Won't you come in?"

"Not now. On my rounds. See you this evening."

He gave her a sunny smile and waved and walked off down the lane.

Agatha retreated to the kitchen. Her knees were trembling. Remember your age, snarled the voice in her head. Agatha ignored it and lit another cigarette while she planned what to wear. No more sensible clothes. She did not stop to consider what gossip the curate had heard that had prompted him to ask her to dinner. Agatha considered herself a very important person, which was her way of lacquering-over her feelings of inferiority.

By the time she stepped out into the balmy summer evening some hours later in a gold silk dress, the bedroom behind her in the cottage was a wreck of discarded clothes. The dress was a plain shirt-waister, Agatha having decided that full evening rig would not be suitable for dinner in a village cottage.

She kept her face averted as she passed the vicarage and knocked at Mrs. Feathers's door. She had not told Mrs. Bloxby about the invitation, feeling that lady would not approve.

Old Mrs. Feathers answered the door. She was grey-haired and stooped and had a mild, innocent face. "Just go on upstairs," she said.

Agatha mounted the narrow cottage stairs. Tristan opened a door at the top. "Welcome," he said. "How nice and cool you look."

He ushered Agatha into a small room where a table had been laid with a white cloth for dinner.

"We'll start right away," he said. He opened the door and shouted down the stairs, "You can start serving now, Mrs. Feathers."

"Doesn't she need some help?" asked Agatha anxiously.

"Oh, no. Don't spoil her fun. She likes looking after me."

But Agatha felt awkward as Mrs. Feathers subsequently

appeared carrying a heavy tray. She laid out two plates of pâté de foie gras, toast melba, a chilled bottle of wine and two glasses. "Just call when you're ready for your next course," she said.

Agatha sat down. Mrs. Feathers spread a large white napkin on Agatha's lap before creaking off.

Tristan poured wine and sat down opposite her. "Now," he said, "tell me what brings a sophisticated lady like yourself to a Cotswold village?"

Agatha told him that she had always had a dream of living in a Cotswold village. She left out the bit about taking early retirement because she did not want to refer to her age. And all the time she talked and ate, she admired the beauty of the curate opposite. He had the face of an angel come to earth with his cherubic, almost androgynous face framed by his gold curls, but his athletic, well-formed body was all masculine.

Tristan rose and called for the second course. Mrs. Feathers appeared bearing tournedos Rossini, new potatoes and salad.

"Isn't Mrs. Feathers an excellent cook?" said Tristan when they were alone again.

"Very," said Agatha. "This steak is excellent. Where did you buy it?"

"I leave all the shopping to Mrs. Feathers. I told her to make a special effort."

"She didn't pay for all this, I hope?"

"Mrs. Feathers insists on paying for my food."

Agatha looked at him uneasily. Surely an old widow like Mrs. Feathers could not afford all this expensive food and wine. But Tristan seemed to take it as his due and he continued to question her about her life until the steak was finished and Mrs. Feathers brought in baked Alaska.

"I've talked about nothing but myself," said Agatha ruefully. "I don't know a thing about you."

"Nothing much to know," said Tristan.

"Where were you before you came down here?"

"At a church in New Cross in London. I ran a boys' club there, you know, get them off the streets. It was going well until I was attacked."

"What on earth happened?"

"One of the gang leaders felt I was taking his members away. Five of them jumped me one night when I was walking home. I was badly beaten up, cracked ribs, all that. To tell the truth, I had a minor nervous breakdown and I felt a spell in the country would be just what I needed."

"How awful for you," said Agatha.

"I'm over it now. These things happen."

"What made you want to join the church?"

"I felt I could help people."

"And are you happy here?"

"I don't think Mr. Bloxby likes me. I think he's a bit jealous."

"He's a difficult man. I'm afraid he doesn't like me either." Both of them laughed, drawn together by the vicar's dislike of both of them.

"You were saying you had been involved in some detection. Tell me about that?"

So Agatha bragged away happily over dessert, over coffee, until, noticing it was nearly midnight, she reluctantly said she should leave.

"Before you go," he said, "I have a talent for playing the stock exchange. I make fortunes for others. Want me to help you?"

"I've got a very good stockbroker," said Agatha. "But I'll let you know."

Somehow, she expected him to offer to walk her home,

but he led the way downstairs and then stood facing her at the bottom. "My turn next time," said Agatha.

"I'll keep you to that." He bent and kissed her gently on the mouth. She stared up at him, dazed. He opened the door. "Good night, Agatha."

"Good night, Tristan," she said faintly.

The door shut behind her. Over at the vicarage, Mrs. Bloxby's face appeared briefly at an upstairs window and then disappeared.

Agatha walked home sedately although she felt like running and jumping and cheering.

It was only when she reached her cottage that she realized she had not set a date for another dinner. She did not even know his phone number. She searched the phone book until she found a listing for Mrs. Feathers. He would not be asleep already. She dialled. Mrs. Feathers answered the phone. Agatha asked to speak to Tristan and waited anxiously.

Then she heard his voice. "Yes?"

"This is Agatha. We forgot to set a date for dinner."

There was a silence. Then he gave a mocking little laugh and said, "Keen, aren't you? I'll let you know."

"Good night," said Agatha quickly and dropped the receiver like a hot potato.

She walked slowly into her kitchen and sat down at the table, her face flaming with mortification.

"You silly old fool," said the voice in her head, and for once Agatha sadly agreed.

Her first feeling when she awoke the next day was that she never wanted to see the curate again. She felt he had led her on to make a fool of herself. A wind had got up and rattled through the dry thatch on the roof overhead and sent small dust devils dancing down Lilac Lane outside. She forced herself to get out of bed and face the day ahead. What if Tristan was joking with Mrs. Bloxby about her? She made herself her customary breakfast of black coffee and decided to fill up the watering cans and water the garden as the radio had announced a hose-pipe ban. She was half-way down the garden when she heard sirens rending the quiet of the village. She slowly put down the watering can and stood, listening. The sirens swept past the end of Lilac Lane and up in the direction of the church and stopped.

Agatha dropped the watering can and fled through the house and out into the lane. Her flat sandals sending up spirals of dust; she ran on in the direction of the vicarage. Please God, she prayed, let it not be Mrs. Bloxby.

There were three police cars and an ambulance. A crowd was gathering. Agatha saw John Fletcher, the landlord from the Red Lion and asked him, "Is someone hurt? What's happened?"

"I don't know," he said.

They waited a long time. Hazy clouds covered the hot sun overhead. The wind had died and all was still. Rumour buzzed through the crowd. It was the vicar, it was Mrs. Bloxby, it was the curate.

A stone-faced policeman was on duty outside the vicarage. He refused to answer questions, simply saying, "Move along there. Nothing to see."

A white-coated forensic unit arrived. People began to drift off. "I'd better open up," said the publican. "We'll find out sooner or later."

Agatha was joined by John Armitage. "What's going on?" he asked.

"I don't know," said Agatha. "I'm terrified something's happened to Mrs. Bloxby."

Then Agatha's friend, Detective Sergeant Bill Wong, came out of the vicarage accompanied by a policewoman.

"Bill!" called Agatha.

"Later," he said. He and the policewoman went to Mrs. Feathers's small cottage and knocked at the door. The old lady opened the door to them. They said something. She put a trembling hand up to her mouth and they disappeared inside and shut the door.

"There's your answer," said John Armitage.

"It's the curate and he's dead because that ambulance hasn't moved!"

# TWO

✝

JOHN and Agatha decided to go back to Agatha's cottage and then return to the vicarage later.

"Who would want to kill the curate—if it was the curate," asked John.

Me, thought Agatha. I could have killed him last night.

Aloud, she said, "I hate this waiting." Then she thought, they'll have questioned Mrs. Feathers and she'll tell them about that dinner last night. I don't want John to know about it. I've got to get rid of him.

"I'm restless," she said, getting to her feet. "I think I'll go for a walk."

"Good idea."

"Alone."

"Oh, all right."

They walked together to the door. Agatha opened it. Detective Inspector Wilkes of the Mircester CID stood there, accompanied by Bill Wong and a policewoman.

"May we come in?" asked Wilkes.

"Yes," said Agatha, flustered. "See you later, John."

He was urged on his way by a push in the back from Agatha.

Agatha led the police into her living-room and sat down feeling, irrationally, like a guilty schoolgirl.

"What's happened?" she asked.

"Mr. Delon, the curate, was found this morning in the vicar's study. He had been stabbed."

Agatha felt hysterical. "Was he stabbed with a rare oriental dagger?" She stifled a giggle.

Wilkes glared at her. "He was stabbed with a paper-knife on the vicar's desk."

Agatha fought down the hysteria. "You can't kill someone with a paper-knife."

"You can with this one. It's very sharp. Mr. Bloxby said he kept it sharp. The church box, the one people put donations in for the upkeep of the church, was lying open. The money had gone."

"I know the vicar took it from the church from time to time to record what had been donated," said Agatha. "But Mr. Delon couldn't have surprised a burglar. I don't think there were ever any donations in there worth bothering about."

"Evidently, according to the vicar, there were this time. The curate had delivered a sermon the Sunday before last about the importance of donating to the upkeep of the church. There were several hundred pounds in there. The vicar hadn't got around to counting it. He says he just checked inside and planned to get down to counting the takings today."

"But what was Mr. Delon doing in the vicar's study?" asked Agatha.

"If we can stop the speculation and get to your movements, Mrs. Raisin. You had dinner with Mr. Delon in his flat last night. You left around midnight."

"Yes."

"Were you intimate with him?"

Agatha's face flamed. "Of course not! I barely knew the man."

"And yet he asked you for dinner."

"Oh, I thought it was a parish thing. I assume it was his way of getting to know everybody."

"So what did you talk about?"

"He was a good listener," said Agatha. "I'm afraid I talked mostly about myself. I asked him about himself and he said he had been at a church in New Cross in London and that he had formed a boys' club and that one of the gang leaders had become angry, thinking he was taking the youth of the area away and had had him beaten up. He said he'd had a nervous breakdown."

"And you left at midnight and that was that?"

"Of course."

"Do you know of any other women in the village he was particularly friendly with?"

"No. I mean, I'd been away and then I was up in London, working. The first time I met him was on Sunday, outside the church. Then he turned up on my doorstep yesterday and invited me to dinner."

"Let's go over it again," said Wilkes.

Agatha went through the whole business again and then felt her face going red. They would check phone calls to Mrs.

Feathers's phone and would know she had phoned him when she got home.

"What is it?" demanded Wilkes, studying her red face.

"When I got home, I realized I had asked him for dinner but hadn't fixed a date, so I phoned him and he said he would let me know."

"Those were his only words?"

"Exactly," said Agatha with all the firmness of one used to lying.

"That will be all for the moment. We would like you to come down to headquarters and sign a statement, say, tomorrow morning, and to hold yourself in readiness for further questioning."

As they rose to leave, Agatha's friend, Detective Sergeant Bill Wong, gave her the ghost of a wink.

"Call me later," mouthed Agatha silently.

As Wilkes was leaving, Agatha called, "When was Mr. Delon killed?"

He turned. "We don't know. Mrs. Bloxby rose at six-thirty this morning. She went out into the garden and noticed the French windows to the study were wide open. She could see papers were blowing about. She went in to close the window and found the curate dead."

Agatha felt a great wave of relief. She realized she had been afraid the vicar might have lost his temper and struck out at Tristan.

"So someone came in from outside?"

"Or someone made it look that way."

Agatha sat down shakily when they had left. Then she rose and phoned the vicarage. A policeman answered and said curtly that neither the vicar nor his wife were free to come to the phone.

The doorbell rang and she rushed to answer it. For once John Armitage got a warm welcome. "Oh, John," cried Agatha, grabbing his arm and dragging him indoors. "Isn't this too awful? Do you think Alf did it and made it look like a burglary?"

"I cannot believe our vicar would harm a fly," said John, shutting the door behind them. "Let's sit down calmly and think about it. Why did the police want to see you?"

"As far as they know, I was the last one to see Tristan alive. I went to his place for dinner and left around midnight."

"Oho. He's a fast worker. How did that come about?"

"He just turned up on the doorstep and asked me, just like that."

"Tell me about it."

"I've already gone over and over it with the police." She started to describe her evening again.

"Wait a minute," he interrupted. "Mrs. Feathers supplied a dinner of pâté de foie gras, tournedos Rossini, and baked Alaska. She can't be rich and she's a widow. Didn't you think it was a bit much of him?"

"I did a bit," said Agatha ruefully.

"Sounds a bit of a taker to me. Did he try to get money out of you?"

"You do underrate my charms, don't you? Oh, Lord. I've just remembered something. He said something about being a whiz at playing the stock exchange and that he could invest money for me. I said I'd a very good stockbroker but that I'd let him know."

"So *that* was why he asked you for dinner."

"What do you mean?" demanded Agatha huffily.

"Look at it this way. He'd conned old Mrs. Feathers into supplying an expensive meal. Who knows? He may have got his hands on her savings. You know what the gossip in this village is like. He'd have heard you're rich. You've got a bit of a reputation when it comes to men."

"Undeserved," snapped Agatha.

"And you're a divorcée. You should tell the police."

"Must I?" asked Agatha bleakly.

"Yes, of course. And just think. They're probably still up at the vicarage and it'll be an excuse for us to get in there."

The policeman on guard at the door of the vicarage listened to Agatha's request to see Wilkes because she had something to tell him relevant to the murder. He disappeared indoors and reappeared a few minutes later. "Follow me," he said. "They're in the garden." The vicar's study door was standing open. Men in white overalls were swarming all over the place.

They followed the policeman out through the French windows and into the garden where Wilkes, a policewoman, the vicar and Mrs. Bloxby sat round a garden table. There was no sign of Bill Wong.

Mrs. Bloxby was holding her husband's hand. Both looked strained.

"What is it?" asked Wilkes.

Agatha drew up a chair and sat down. She told him about the expensive dinner and about the offer to invest money for her.

"This might give us an angle," said Wilkes slowly. "He may have been successful with some of the other women. We'll be checking his bank account. Now Mrs. Feathers says you were the only one he invited home for dinner and he told her to make a special effort and you were very rich and probably used to the best."

Agatha felt herself grow red yet again with mortification.

Wilkes turned to Mrs. Bloxby. "Was he particularly friendly with any other women in the village?"

"It's hard to say," she said wearily. "I think they mostly invited him for meals. Miss Jellop was one. Then there was Peggy Slither over in Ancombe. Oh dear, let me think. Old Colonel Tremp's widow, Mrs. Tremp, she lives up the hill out of the village in that converted barn. So many were smitten with him. He was very handsome."

"And what about the both of you? Did he offer to invest any money?"

"No, he said he had a little money from a family trust. He didn't ask us for any."

"How come you got him as a curate?" asked Agatha.

"I was told he'd had a nervous breakdown," said the vicar. "I was glad of help in the parish work."

"And did you find him helpful?" asked Wilkes.

"The first week was fine. But then he became—selective."

"What do you mean—selective?"

"I found he had not been calling on any of the elderly or sick, unless—I now realize—they were wealthy. I took him to task for neglect of duty and he simply smiled and said of course he would attend to it. Then I fell ill and he took over the services in the church. I felt it churlish of me to dislike him—for I was beginning to dislike him—and I feared I was envious of the way he could pack the church."

"It looks as if he might have surprised a burglar," said Wilkes.

"Or," interrupted Agatha suddenly, "been robbing the cash box himself."

"If he had a private income and if, as we fear, he had been taking money from gullible women, why would he want a few hundred pounds?"

"He was very vain," said Mrs. Bloxby. "It was because of his sermon that there was such a large donation. I think he probably saw that money as rightly his."

"And he had a key to the vicarage," said Wilkes, who had already established that fact. "Those long windows into the study, do you keep them locked?"

Mrs. Bloxby looked guilty. "We do try to remember to lock them, but sometimes we forget. Up until recently, we never bothered to lock up at night, but with the police station having been closed down along with all the other local stations, there have been a lot of burglaries recently."

"So far, we can't find any sign of a break-in and no fingerprints at all, not even the vicar's," said Wilkes. "Excuse me, I'll see how they're getting on. Come with me, Reverend, and check again to see if there is anything else missing."

The vicar, the policewoman, and Wilkes went indoors. "Is there anything I can do for you?" asked Agatha, taking Mrs. Bloxby's hand in hers. "You've helped me so much in the past when horrible things have happened to me."

"You can find out who did it," said Mrs. Bloxby. "Because they suspect Alf. You see, a lot of the women were smitten by Mr. Delon, and before he died, there was a lot of talk about how Alf should step down and leave the sermons to Mr. Delon. My husband," she sighed, "can be, well, not very tactful and when Miss Jellop suggested such an arrangement to him, he told her not to be such a silly woman. The police are already beginning to think that Alf was jealous of Mr. Delon. He was in bed with me when the murder took place and so I told them, but they look at me in that way which seems to say, 'You would say that.'"

"We'll do our best," said John. Agatha looked at him in surprise. She had forgotten he was there. A man as good-looking as John had no right to be so forgettable.

"I think," pursued John, "that we should start off with whichever church he was at in New Cross in London before he came down here."

"But the police will dig all that up," protested Agatha.

"I still think we might be able to find out things the police don't know. They'll be sticking to facts. We can find out if he conned any of the women in New Cross out of money. One of them could have been watching Mrs. Feathers's cottage and seen him slip out. She may have entered the study by the French windows. There's no flower-bed in front of the windows to leave footprints, only grass."

"It all sounds far-fetched to me," said Agatha crossly, cross because she expected everyone at all times to play Dr. Watson to her Sherlock Holmes. "I mean, what sort of person would watch the cottage all night?"

"A jealous, furious woman," said John. "Come on, Agatha, don't knock it down just because it wasn't your idea. We'll hang around another day to be available for the police and then we'll go off."

"I think that's a very good idea," said Mrs. Bloxby quietly.

"All right," said Agatha sulkily. Mrs. Bloxby, despite her fear for her husband and her shock at the murder, could not help but feel amused. There was something childlike about Agatha Raisin with her bearlike eyes under a heavy fringe of glossy brown hair registering a pouting disappointment that someone else was getting in on the act.

"Now, have you eaten?" asked Agatha. "I've got some microwave meals at home I could bring along."

"No, thank you," said the vicar's wife. "Neither of us feels like eating." She privately thought that even if she and her husband had been starving, they could not have faced one of Agatha's shop-bought frozen meals.

Agatha lit a cigarette. "Agatha!" exclaimed Mrs. Bloxby, startled into the use of Agatha's first name. "You're smoking again!"

"Tastes all right now," mumbled Agatha.

John produced a small notebook. "I'll just make a note of these women who were close to Tristan. Let me see—there was a Miss Jellop, and then there were two others."

"Peggy Slither and Mrs. Tremp," said Mrs. Bloxby.

"You call her Peggy?" asked Agatha. "First name?"

"She is not a member of the ladies' society."

"What's she like and where does she live?" asked John.

"In Ancombe. A cottage called Shangri-la."

"That's a bit twee."

"I think she means it to be a sort of joke. She finds it fashionable to adopt the unfashionable. She has gnomes in her garden. That sort of thing. Rather loud and busty. About fifty. Her money comes from fish and chips. She never married. Her father had a profitable chain of fish and chip shops and she sold them when her father died."

"I know Miss Jellop," snapped Agatha, who did not like John's taking over the investigation.

Mrs. Bloxby leaned back and closed her eyes.

"We'd better go," said John.

"Phone me if there is anything I can do," said Agatha.

Mrs. Bloxby opened her eyes. "Just find out who did it."

When John and Agatha arrived back at Agatha's cottage it was to find Bill Wong waiting outside for them. "Thought I'd drop in for a chat. Trust you to land in trouble again, Agatha."

Agatha unlocked the door. "Come in and we'll have coffee in the garden."

Bill Wong was Agatha's first friend, a young police detective, half Chinese and half English. When they were seated in the garden, he surveyed Agatha with his brown slanting eyes. "I know you've already made a statement, but I'd like to know a bit more about your evening with Tristan. Did he come on to you?"

"Well, he kissed me."

"And didn't that let you know there was something funny about him?" demanded John sharply. "I mean, the difference in ages and all that."

"I have attracted younger men before," said Agatha waspishly.

"So he kissed you. When?" asked Bill.

"When I was leaving."

"What sort of kiss? Social peck?"

"No, a warm one, on the lips. What's all this about?"

"It's this money business. He was after money, we think. I wondered how far he was prepared to go. If he'd had a full-blown affair with any of them, that might have been a reason for murder."

"He didn't have an affair with me," said Agatha. "I'd have sussed him out sooner or later. I'm not *stupid,* you know."

"Women can become very stupid faced with such beauty. I saw him preach. My girl-friend heard all about him and dragged me along to church."

"Girl-friend?" Agatha was momentarily distracted.

"Alice. Alice Bryan. She works as a teller in Lloyds bank in Mircester."

"Serious?"

"It always is," said Bill sadly.

And it'll be over like a shot when she meets your parents, thought Agatha. Bill's parents could repel any girl-friend.

"Anyway," said Bill briskly, "what did you talk about?"

"Me, mostly," said Agatha ruefully. "When I realized it was all about me and nothing about him, I asked him about himself. He told me about working in New Cross and forming a boys' club and how the gang leaders thought they were losing members because of him. Five of them had attacked him one night and injured him and then he had a nervous breakdown."

"Which church in New Cross was it?" asked John.

"Saint Edmund's. Here! I don't want you pair poking your nose in and interfering with police work."

"As if we would," said Agatha, flashing John a warning look.

"What did you think of Tristan when you heard him preach?" John asked Bill.

"I thought him stupid and vain and the sermon was a load of nothing. On the other hand, I could have been jealous. Alice was gazing at him as if an angel had come to earth. So, Agatha, he didn't try to persuade you in any determined way to let him have money?"

"No, apart from suggesting he could invest some for me, he let the subject drop."

"Strikes me as odd from the little I know of him. Any suggestion of a future dinner date?"

"No!" Agatha flushed angrily. Bill eyed her shrewdly.

"He got Mrs. Feathers to go to a lot of trouble producing an expensive dinner and nothing came of it. I'll bet he thought you were a waste of space."

"If he thought so, he didn't tell me."

"We'll find out more when we study his bank account and find out who's been giving him money, and if he invested any of it, I'll eat my hat."

"It still seems odd, this idea of someone watching the cottage during the night and then following Tristan to the vicarage," said John. "If he'd cheated old Mrs. Feathers and she'd just found out about it, she could have heard him going out and followed him. The old sleep lightly."

"I can't see old Mrs. Feathers at her age going to tackle a young man like that."

"She could simply have meant to berate him if she found him taking the church money," pursued John, "and seized that letter opener and stabbed him. I mean, how many people would know that letter opener was so sharp? Did you, Agatha?"

"I was there one day talking to Mrs. Bloxby when he came in carrying the post. He was slicing open the letters and I remember thinking then that the letter opener must have been sharp. It was a silver one in the shape of a dagger. Not a real dagger."

"And what about the vicar himself?" asked John quietly. "I mean, he could have caught him at it. Was there any sign of a struggle?"

"No, Tristan was stabbed with one blow to the back of the neck."

"Yes, that would take a lot of force," said Agatha.

"Not necessarily," said Bill. "As the knife was sharp, once the skin was penetrated then the blade would sink in easily and it was sunk in up to the haft. Rather like stabbing a melon. But we'll know more after the post-mortem."

"I read somewhere," said John, "that victims of stab wounds don't often die immediately. Say the vicar did it, not in his study but at Tristan's. Wonder if he has a key to that cottage? Anyway, some people stabbed with a sharp thin blade can walk around for a couple of hours afterwards. Say the vicar stabbed Tristan and Tristan doesn't know how bad he's hurt. So he decides to clear off, but first of all, he's going to get that money out of the cash box and take it with him and he collapses in the vicar's study."

Agatha gave him an impatient look. "With the knife still in his neck?"

"Maybe he knew it was safer to leave it in until he got to a hospital."

"Oh, really? And some doctor looks at the knife in the back of his neck and promptly calls the police."

"Oh, shut up, you two," said Bill. "That's where amateurs

are such a menace. Stick to the facts, to what you know."

But John, undeterred, volunteered, "Maybe Alf Bloxby summoned him and made it look as if Tristan was robbing the church box."

"You're forgetting Mrs. Bloxby," said Agatha. "She would never cover up for her husband if he'd committed a murder."

"But she might not have known. They both probably claim to have slept through the whole business, but maybe she was heavily asleep."

"I've had enough," said Bill. "I'm off. Agatha, report to police headquarters tomorrow morning and sign a statement."

Agatha was driving the next morning. "Look out for that child on a bicycle!" shouted John at one point and at another, "You're going too fast."

Agatha sighed. "This is like a marriage without the nookie."

"May I point out that no sex was your choice?"

Agatha stared at him.

"Look at the road, Agatha, for God's sake!"

"What is up with you, John? You're usually so . . . so *placid*. Now you're bitching and whining like an old grump."

"I made some reasonable suggestions to Bill Wong yesterday and all you did was sneer."

"I thought they were a bit far-fetched. I'm entitled to my opinion."

"You could have told me afterwards. Look, Agatha. We are both amateurs at this game. There is no need to go on as if I am some sort of office boy."

"I never . . . Oh, let's drop the whole thing. I don't want to quarrel."

They continued in an uneasy silence.

After Agatha had made her statement, John said, "We should start off by going straight to New Cross."

"What? Right away?"

"Why not?"

"Oh, all right. But I don't like driving up to London."

"Then I'll drive, if your insurance covers me. Unless, of course, you have to be in the driver's seat all the time, both literally and metaphorically."

"Drive if you like," said Agatha huffily. "My insurance does cover you driving."

What had come over him? wondered Agatha, as they drove towards London. She was used to a rather colourless John. He had been going on as if he thought she was bossy. Like most high-powered people with a soft, shivering interior, Agatha considered herself a gentle lady, sensitive and sympathetic.

But by the time they reached New Cross, the driving seemed to have soothed John and he appeared to have reverted to his usual equable self. Probably his bad mood was nothing to do with me, thought Agatha. I don't upset people. Must have been someone or something else and he took it out on me.

John stopped the car and asked directions to St. Edmund's until he found a man who actually knew where the church was.

St. Edmund's was in a leafy backstreet. It was a Victorian building, still black from the soot of former coal-burning decades. White streaks of pigeon droppings cut through the soot up at the roof. It had four crenellated spires with weather vanes of gold pennants. Beside the church was a Victorian villa, also black with soot, which, they guessed, must be the vicarage.

John pressed the old-fashioned brass bell-push sunk into the stone wall beside the door.

The door was opened after a few moments by a heavy-set woman with her hair wound up in pink plastic rollers. She had a massive bosom under an overall and a large, truculent red face.

"Whatissit?"

"We would like to see the vicar," said John.

" 'Sinerstudy."

"Would you mind telling him we're here?"

Without asking them who they were, the woman shuffled off. "Poor man," murmured John. "What a housekeeper!"

The vicar arrived and peered at them curiously. He had what Agatha always thought of as a Church of England face: weak eyes behind thick glasses, sparse grey hair, grey skin, a bulbous nose and a fleshy mouth with thick pale lips.

"What do you want to see me about?" he asked. His voice was beautiful, the old Oxford accent, so pleasant to listen to that it sounds like no accent at all.

"I am Agatha Raisin and this is John Armitage. We both live in Carsely and are friends of the vicar there, Mr. Alfred Bloxby."

"Oh, dear." His face creased up in distress. "I heard about that dreadful murder on the news this morning. Terrible, terrible. How do you do. I am Fred Lancing. Do come in."

He led them into the study, a shabby book-lined room. "I should really take you through to the sitting-room," he said apologetically, "but I only really use this room and the others are rather damp and dusty. Would you like tea?"

"Yes, please," said Agatha.

He opened the door of the study and shouted, "Mrs. Buggy!"

"What yer want?" came the answering shout.

"Tea for three."

"Think I've got nothing better ter do?"

"Just do it!" shouted the vicar, turning pink.

He came back and sat down behind his desk. Agatha and

John sat side by side on an old black horsehair sofa. "It was those evening classes on feminism," he sighed. "Mrs. Buggy was much taken with them. She has regarded me as a tyrant ever since. How can I help you? Poor Tristan."

Agatha outlined what had happened and said they were afraid that the police suspected Mr. Bloxby and she and John wanted to help to clear his name.

The police called on me yesterday evening," said the vicar mildly. "But I really couldn't tell them anything much."

"Did Tristan really get beaten up by a gang and have a nervous breakdown?" asked Agatha.

"I gather that is what he said."

At that moment, the door crashed open and Mrs. Buggy entered with three cups of milky tea on a tray, which she crashed down on the vicar's desk.

"No biscuits," she snarled on her road out.

"I do hate bossy women," murmured the vicar.

"I do so agree with you," said John, flashing a look at Agatha.

"I did not know the vicar of Carsely—Mr. Bloxby, did you say?—was under suspicion."

"I'm afraid so," said Agatha. "Please tell us the truth about Tristan Delon. It could help. Someone murdered him and it could be someone from his past."

The vicar stood up and handed each of them a cup of tea before retreating behind his desk.

"I am wondering what to tell you," he said. "You see, if I tell you more than I have told the police, they will be very angry."

"I am a private detective," said Agatha. "I will not tell the police anything you say. I promise."

"I, I, I," murmured John, and Agatha threw him a fulminating look.

"De mortuis . . ." said the vicar. "I always think it is cruel to speak ill of the dead."

"But surely it is necessary if it can help bring justice to the living. I gather Tristan was gay," said John. Agatha stared at him in amazement.

"I believe so," said Mr. Lancing. "There are so many temptations in town for a young man."

"What temptations?" demanded Agatha sharply.

"He bragged about having a rich businessman as a friend and showed off a gold Rolex. But his homosexuality was not the problem. He should really have gone on the stage. He was very flamboyant in the pulpit. He charmed the parishioners—at first."

"And then what happened?" asked John.

"He seemed to become bored after he had been with me for a few weeks. It was then he developed a, well, nasty streak. He would find out some parishioner's vulnerable point and lean on it, if you know what I mean."

"Blackmail?" demanded Agatha eagerly.

"No, no. Just . . . well, to put it in one word . . . spite."

"Do you know the name of this businessman?" asked John.

There was a long silence, and then the vicar said, "No, although he bragged, he was very secretive about the details."

He does know who it is, thought John.

Agatha sat forward on the sofa, her bearlike eyes glistening. "So he didn't have a nervous breakdown. He didn't get beaten up."

"He did get beaten up."

"Because of his boys' club?"

"He didn't have a boys' club. He appeared very frightened, however. He said he had to get away. He seemed to become quite demented. He was also very penitent and said he wanted to make a new start. I made inquiries and hit on the idea of removing him to a quiet country village. He had done nothing criminal, you see. And he did seem determined to become a better person."

"Did he have any particular friend in the parish?"

"He did have one, Sol MacGuire, a builder. He lives over the shops on Briory Road. Number sixteen. It's just around the corner if you turn left when you leave the vicarage."

Agatha rounded on John as soon as they had left the vicarage. "How did you know he was gay?"

"I didn't. It was just a wild guess."

"Humph!"

"And I'll bet he knows the name of that businessman."

"He wouldn't lie."

"Because he's a vicar? Come *on,* Agatha. You can be surprisingly naïve at times."

"I don't believe you," said Agatha furiously.

They walked in silence round the corner to Briory Road. It was a shabbier street with smaller houses. Number 16 had an excuse for a front garden: a sagging privet hedge, a broken bicycle, rank grass and weeds.

No one answered their knock. They tried the neighbours and were told he was probably out working but that he usually came home around six in the evening.

"Four hours to kill," said John, looking at his watch. "But we haven't eaten anything. Let's find a pub."

They found one out in the main road where traffic shimmered in the heat. John pushed open the door and they walked into the gloom. It was fairly empty. It was an old-fashioned London pub which had not yet been "bistro-fied" like many others. Sunlight shone dimly through the dusty windows. Fruit machines winked and blinked. But at least there was no pipe-in Muzak. The landlord, a thin, sour man, said lunches were over but that he could make them some sandwiches. They ordered ham sandwiches and beer and when their order arrived, retreated to a corner table.

"At least we're a bit ahead of the police," said Agatha.

"Only a bit ahead. They'll be back again sometime to ask the vicar more questions, and having told us, he'll probably now tell them."

"Do you really think so? He might not want to tell them now and let them know he was withholding informations in the first place."

"Maybe. These sandwiches are awful. I haven't had pub sandwiches like these in years. The ham is slimy and the bread's dry."

"Keeping up the good old English pub traditions," said Agatha gloomily.

"This news about the rich man is interesting, though," said John. "I mean, if he's really someone important, he might have wanted to get rid of Tristan. Maybe Tristan was blackmailing him."

"We forgot to ask how long it was between Tristan leaving New Cross and Tristan arriving in Carsely."

"How would that help?"

"If it was a long period, he might not have that much left in his bank account. You see, he wasn't in Carsely long enough to fleece anyone to any significant degree. I think he liked to spend money on himself. Whatever he had got, he might have dissipated so his bank account won't give much of a clue."

"It will," said John, "if it shows cheques from any of the villagers, or from this businessman, whoever he is."

They debated the mystery and then left the pub and wandered around the streets of New Cross, past Indian shops and Turkish restaurants until John looked at his watch and said, "Time to go back to see if Sol MacGuire is at home."

# THREE

✝

SOL MacGuire was another Adonis, but a black-haired, blue-eyed one. He looked shocked when they told him they were investigating the murder of Tristan Delon.

"Sure, now, isn't that the big shock you've given me," he said. "Come on in."

They followed him into a small living-room which seemed to be full of old beer cans and old copies of newspapers and magazines.

"Find a space and sit yourselves down," said Sol. "How was he murdered? I haven't kept up with the news."

John told him and then asked what he knew about Tristan. "Not that much," said Sol. "He saw me working on a local building site and kept coming round to chat. I told him flat-out I wasn't gay and he just laughed and said he wasn't gay either."

"I couldn't be bothered much with him at first, but he kept coming round. He was funny in a malicious way, know what I mean?"

"Give us an example?" asked Agatha.

"He was adored by the women in the parish, but he seemed to despise them."

"Anyone in particular?"

"He'd talk about a Mrs. Hill. Said she used to look at him like a dog. He said he felt like snapping his fingers and tossing her a biscuit. Things like that."

Agatha leaned forward. "Did Tristan ever talk about some businessman, someone who gave him presents?"

"Oh, that. Mind if I get myself a beer?"

"Go ahead."

"Want one?"

"Not for me," said John. "I've already had some beer and I'm driving. What about you, Agatha?"

"Not for me either."

Sol disappeared and returned after a few moments with a can of beer which he popped open. After a hearty swig, he wiped his mouth with the back of his hand and said, "He showed me a gold Rolex. Said it was a present from Richard Binser."

Agatha's eyes opened wide in amazement. "Richard Binser, the tycoon?"

"That's what he said. But then, he was a terrible liar."

"Do you know who beat him up?"

"He said it was one of the gangs, but he didn't know any gangs. Trust me. Maybe one of them women got wise to him and took a club to him. I dunno."

"Do you know where this Mrs. Hill lives?"

"He told me. It's a big house round in Jeves Place. You cross the main road, take Gladstone Street, turn right on Palmerston, then first left is Jeves. Don't know the number, but it's a big place on its own. I'm curious, like," went on Sol, his accent an odd mixture of Irish and south London. "Why ask questions around here, and why you? You his relatives?"

"No," said Agatha. "We are private detectives."

"Got a licence?"

"Pending," lied Agatha.

"Well, good luck to you. But if he was murdered in that village, stands to reason someone down there killed him."

"Do you know how long it was," asked Agatha, "between the attack and him leaving here?"

"He came round once after the attack. Said he was going abroad. Would be about six months ago."

"That long!"

"See what I mean?" said Sol. "He was old history far as New Cross was concerned."

When they left Sol, Agatha said, "Let's go after Binser."

"It's late. We can find his offices—I think they're in Cheapside in the City. As we're here, shouldn't we try Mrs. Hill?"

"All right, though mark my words, she'll just turn out to be a sad middle-aged woman, duped by Tristan."

"Like you," murmured John.

Agatha glared at him and stalked on in an angry silence.

When they found the villa in Jeves Place, it appeared there was no one at home. Far in the distance came the menacing rumble of thunder.

"I think we should leave things for tonight," said John, "drive back to Carsely and try Binser tomorrow and then Mrs. Hill."

Agatha agreed because she was tired.

The storm burst halfway to Carsely and John had to drive very slowly through the torrents of rain. As he turned at last into the road leading down into Carsely, the storm clouds rolled

43

away. He opened the car window and a chilly little breeze blew in.

"End of summer," said Agatha. "What time do we set off in the morning?"

"Early. About six-thirty. Beat the rush. Don't groan. We'll take my car and you can sleep on the road up to town if you're still tired."

Agatha said good night to him when they reached Lilac Lane. Her cats came to meet her, yawning and purring. She fed them and then put a lasagne—Mama Livia's Special—in the microwave.

After she had eaten, she bathed and went to bed. Before she went to sleep, she fought down nagging jabs of conscience that were telling her that she should have phoned Bill Wong and brought him up-to-date on what they had found.

"If Binser is in his office, we'll be lucky," said John as he joined the traffic heading for London on the M25 the next morning. "He travels a lot."

"Maybe we should have waited at home and phoned him," said Agatha sleepily.

"Best to surprise him."

"How are we going to get past all the minions he'll surely have to protect him?"

"We'll send in a note saying we want to see him about Tristan Delon."

"And if he doesn't see us?"

"Oh, do shut up, Agatha. We have to try."

"It will be difficult," pursued Agatha. "I remember seeing pictures of him in *Celeb* magazine. Wife and two children."

"Like I said, we must try."

Richard Binser's offices were in an impressive modern

building of steel and glass with a great tree growing up to the glass roof from the entrance hall.

"Here goes," said Agatha, marching up to the long reception desk where four beautiful and fashionably thin young ladies were answering phones.

"Mr. Binser," said Agatha to the one she considered the least intimidating.

"What time is your appointment?"

"We don't have one," said Agatha. She produced a sealed envelope which contained a note she had written in the car. It was marked "Urgent, Private & Confidential." "See that he gets this right away. I am sure he will want to see us."

"Take a seat," said the receptionist, indicating a bank of sofas and chairs over by the entrance doors.

They sat down and waited, and waited.

At last the receptionist they had spoken to approached them and said, "I will take you up. Follow me."

A glass elevator bore them up and up to the top of the building. It opened into another reception area. A middle-aged secretary greeted them and asked them to wait.

Again, they sat down. The receptionist had gone back downstairs and the secretary had retreated through a door leading off the reception. It was very quiet.

Agatha was just beginning to wonder if everyone had forgotten about them, when the secretary came back and said, "Mr. Binser will see you now."

She led them through an inner office and then opened a heavy door leading off it and ushered them into a room where a small, balding man sat behind a large Georgian desk.

He did not rise to meet them, simply surveyed them coldly, then said, "That will be all, Miss Partle. I will call you if I need you."

The secretary left and closed the door behind her.

"Sit!" commanded Richard Binser, indicating two low chairs in front of his desk.

Agatha and John sat down.

"You are not quite what I expected. I am taping this and I warn you both if you try to blackmail me, I will call the police."

"We are not here to blackmail you," said John. "We are investigating the death of Tristan Delon."

"And you are?"

"John Armitage and Agatha Raisin."

"John Armitage. The writer?"

"Yes."

"I've read all your books." The tycoon visibly thawed.

John explained that they both lived in Carsely and were friends of the vicar and anxious to clear his name; that they had learned that Binser had given Tristan presents.

Binser switched off the tape recorder and passed a hand over his forehead. "I thought you were his relatives."

"Was Tristan trying to blackmail you?"

"Oh, yes, but he didn't get anywhere. I may as well tell you what happened. I suppose the police will find out about me eventually. Where shall I begin? I give a lot of money to charities, but my employees sift through the applications, type up a report and I decide how much each should get. Therefore I was a bit taken aback when my senior secretary, Miss Partle, insisted that I should see Tristan in person. It seemed he wanted to raise funds to start a boys' club in New Cross. I was amused that my usually stern secretary appeared to have been bowled over by this Tristan and so I agreed to see him. He was so beautiful and so charming that I began at times to doubt my own sexuality. He flattered me very cleverly. I do not have a son and it amused me to see the way Tristan's eyes lit up when I gave him a present. Then I cut off the friendship."

"Why?" asked Agatha.

"I went down to the church in New Cross one day to find out how the boys' club was getting along. I had given Tristan a cheque for ten thousand pounds to rent a hall and buy equipment. He had asked for more money, but being first and last a businessman, I wanted to see how he had used the money he already had. He was out when I called, but the vicar was there. He said he'd never heard of a boys' club. Tristan came in at that point and waffled and protested that he had meant it to be a surprise but it became clear to me that he had done nothing. I did not want anyone to know how I had been suckered and so I left the vicar to deal with him. Then Tristan wrote to me, threatening to tell my wife that we'd had an affair—which we most certainly had not—and saying he would show her the presents I had given him. I told him if he approached me again I would go straight to the police and that I'd taped his call. All my calls are taped. I never heard from him again. But I was puzzled at being so easily taken in. I consulted a psychiatrist friend and outlined what I knew of Tristan's character. He asked me if Tristan was fascinated by mirrors. It seemed an odd question, but I remembered that on the few occasions I had taken Tristan out for dinner to a restaurant with a lot of mirrors that he would sit gazing fascinated at his own reflection.

"The psychiatrist said he was probably a somatic narcissist and that this type of narcissist could charm people by exuding that warm, fuzzy emotional feeling of well-being you get on a good day. He said this type could be prone to violence.

"Anyway, that was Tristan's charm. He made me feel good about myself. I was sure, however, that I would hear from him again, but not a word. When I received your note, I thought he had left some journal about our friendship and that you had come to blackmail me. But that's all there was to it. I pride myself on being a good judge of character and yet Tristan had me completely fooled."

"I don't think the police need to know about this," said John, "unless the vicar tells them. We certainly won't. Will we, Agatha?"

Again those jabs of conscience. But Agatha said reluctantly, "No."

"I liked him," said John, as they joined the stream of traffic heading for south London.

"Binser? I suppose."

"You don't seem too sure."

"I had it in my mind that whoever beat him up or had him beaten up had something to do with his murder. A powerful man like Binser could have had him beaten up."

"You've been watching too many left-wing dramas on the box about sinister company executives, Agatha."

"It could have happened that way," said Agatha stubbornly.

A glaring, watery sunlight was bathing London. Agatha glanced sideways at John and noticed for the first time the loosening of the skin under his chin and the network of wrinkles at the side of his eyes. This for some reason made her feel cheerful and she began to whistle tunelessly until John told her to stop.

Back at New Cross, they drove round to Jeves Place and parked in front of the villa. The front door was standing a few inches open. "Someone's at home," said Agatha.

"Good," said John. "Let's go."

A thin voice was singing a hymn somewhere in the interior of the house. John rang the bell. A very small woman with greying hair and a sallow skin came to the door carrying a feather duster.

"Mrs. Hill?" asked Agatha, pushing in front of John who,

she obscurely felt, was taking over too much of this investigation.

"Yes. I am Mrs. Hill."

Agatha introduced both of them and launched into their reasons for wanting to speak to her.

Mrs. Hill stepped out on the doorstep and looked nervously up and down the street. "You'd better come in," she whispered, although the street was empty.

She led them into a large dark room full of heavy old furniture. "I was shocked about poor Tristan's death," she said. "Such a good young man."

"May we sit down?" asked Agatha.

"Oh, please do."

John and Agatha sat in hard high-backed chairs and Mrs. Hill sank down on the edge of an armchair and looked at them with all the fascination of a bird confronted with a snake.

"He wasn't very good at all, as it turns out," said Agatha bluntly. "He conned a respectable businessman out of money to set up a boys' club, and of course he kept the money. No boys' club."

John glared at Agatha and mouthed, "Shut up!" The business about Binser should surely be kept private.

But tears welled up in little Mrs. Hill's eyes and rolled down her cheeks. "I'm so glad I wasn't the only one," she choked out. "I've felt such a fool."

John passed her a large clean handkerchief and she dried her eyes and blew her nose. "Tell us about him," said Agatha gently.

"I felt so silly, so betrayed. You see, I adored him. I saw later what must have happened. All the houses in this street are split up into flats except mine. I have the reputation of being wealthy. I am referred to as the rich Mrs. Hill. But to go back to the beginning. Tristan flattered me. He made me feel good, made me feel worthwhile. I was quite dazed by the impact he had on me. We occasionally went out together, but somewhere where no one would recognize us. He said he didn't want me making the other women of the parish jealous. He said he cared for me. He said that he thought age difference was no barrier when two people respected each other." She wiped away a tear. "I lived and breathed for him. Then he asked me for a donation for this boys' club he said he was setting up. I confided in him that I had no money to spare. I lived on very little. I said I hoped my savings would last until I died. He asked me a lot of questions about how much I was worth, seemingly sympathetically. And then he stopped calling. I thought he loved me," she wailed. "He said he loved me. And I . . . I would have died for him."

She gave a great gulp and then went on. "I waited outside the vicarage one day until I saw him coming out and I asked him why he had been avoiding me. I reminded him he'd said he loved me. He laughed in my face. He said he was gay. He said a lot of things I don't want to repeat. I could have killed him. But I didn't."

"Do you think he did get money out of anyone else?" asked John quietly.

"I don't know. It was, before he came, a tiny congregation. When he preached instead of the vicar, a lot of people came but mostly silly young girls. Please, you won't tell anyone what I've told you. I couldn't bear it."

"We won't unless we have to," said Agatha. "You've got a lot of rooms here, haven't you?"

"Too many," she said in a hollow voice.

"You should let a few rooms out," said Agatha bracingly. "Give you an income."

"But I might get, well, bad people."

"Use an estate agent to handle the renting for you. You couldn't charge all that much because they wouldn't have private kitchens or bathrooms, not unless you spent a lot of money on renovation. I saw an estate agent's out in the main road that handles rentals. They could vet the people for you. Means you wouldn't be alone in this house either. I mean, no children, no pets; just collect the money."

"I couldn't . . ."

"Oh, yes, you could. Look, get your coat and we'll go with you to that estate agent and see what they say."

John Armitage wanted to question the vicar again. The vicar had deliberately lied to them about Richard Binser. He knew Binser because Binser had said he called on him. The vicar had also said that Tristan had done nothing criminal and yet he had. He had pocketed ten thousand pounds. But John had to fret with impatience while Agatha plunged happily into room rentals with Mrs. Hill, who was looking happier by the minute. A representative from the estate agent's then had to come back to the house with them and inspect the rooms. He said for a modest sum she could have wash-basins installed in the bedrooms and allow tenants the use of the kitchen. He seemed as bossy and managing as Agatha Raisin, and Mrs. Hill was delighted to be ordered what to do. When Agatha finally decided she had done enough, a grateful and tearful Mrs. Hill hugged her and said she had given her a new start in life. Agatha said gruffly it was her pleasure, but looked every bit as bored as she was beginning to feel.

"Well, now that waste of space is over," said John crossly, "I want to see that vicar again."

"I had to do something for the poor soul," snapped Agatha.

"That poor soul, as you call her, could have stabbed Tristan. We never asked her what she was doing on the night he was murdered. If you are going to be so trusting about every suspect, we may as well pack it in."

"I'm beginning to think I don't really know you," said Agatha. "You're quite nasty."

"You don't even know yourself, Agatha Raisin."

"Are we going to stand here all day bickering?"

"I want to talk to that vicar again."

"So let's get on with it, for God's sake!"

"I'm tired and we haven't eaten."

"We'll get something after we grill the vicar. But not that pub again."

The vicar of St. Edmund's looked distinctly unhappy to see them again. There was no sign of his ferocious housekeeper.

"I am rather busy writing my sermon," he began.

"We will only take a few minutes of your time, Mr. Lancing," said Agatha. "We want to know why you lied to us."

"Dear me. You'd better come in."

When they were once more seated in his study, Agatha began. "You told us that Tristan had done nothing criminal. Yet he had conned Mr. Binser out of ten thousand pounds. You also told us that you did not know Mr. Binser and yet he said he called on you."

"He did call on me but he urged me not to tell anyone how he had been fooled by Tristan. He said it would be bad for his business image. And Tristan was so truly penitent. He assured me he would pay back every penny."

"Well, we gather he didn't."

"I am sorry I lied to you, but I did give Mr. Binser my solemn word that I would not say anything."

"Is there anything else you have not told us?"

"Not that I can think of." Mr. Lancing gave them a strained look. "Surely what I have told you is enough." His voice became angry. "You are not the police. I should never have spoken to you in the first place. You have no authority."

"We are merely trying to help our local vicar, Mr. Bloxby," said John gently. "Surely you can see that. The police will not hear of anything you have told us unless it is really necessary."

"Then would you mind leaving? You have upset me very much."

"And that's that," said Agatha wearily. "Let's get something to eat."

They stopped at a service station on the A40 for a greasy all-day breakfast of egg, sausage and chips.

"I keep having a feeling we're wasting our time up in London," said John. "The murder was committed in Carsely and I'm sure our murderer lives in the village or round about."

"No, I think the clues lie in London," said Agatha, more out of a desire to contradict John than because she really believed it.

They took to the road again and Agatha fell asleep and did not wake until they were going through Woodstock. "Goodness, have I been asleep all that time?" she said, sitting upright.

"Yes," said John, "and you snored terribly."

"I've had enough of you for one day," snarled Agatha. "You're always nit-picking about something."

"I was merely stating a fact," he said stiffly.

Agatha stifled a yawn and thought longingly of the comfort and peace of her cottage.

When John finally drove into the village, it was to see the narrow main street almost blocked by two television vans.

"I thought the press would have given up by now," said John.

He turned into Lilac Lane. A police car was standing outside Agatha's cottage. "Listen," said John fiercely, "I don't know what's going on, but tell them we simply went up to London for the day to look at the shops and have a meal. No, wait, they'll check restaurants. We can tell them about the service station and then just say we had taken a picnic lunch and ate it in Green Park."

When they parked, Bill Wong and a detective constable and a policewoman got out of the waiting car.

Bill looked grim. "Where were you, Mrs. Raisin?" he demanded. Agatha's heart sank at the formal use of her second name.

"In London, going around the shops," she said. "Why?"

"We'd better go inside," said Bill. "You come along as well, Mr. Armitage."

Agatha unlocked her cottage door. "Come into the kitchen," she said, nearly tripping over her cats, which were winding themselves around her ankles.

When they were all seated around the kitchen table, Agatha said, "What's this about? I've made a statement."

"There has been a further development," said Bill, his eyes hard. Then he winced as Hodge dug his nails into his trouser leg.

"Miss Jellop has been murdered."

# FOUR

†

"HOW? When?" asked Agatha.

"We cannot ascertain the exact time of death at the moment, but sometime early this evening. She was strangled. She lives alone and might not have been found for some time except Mrs. Bloxby went to call on her and found the door open and then found Miss Jellop."

"Poor Mrs. Bloxby!" Agatha half-rose. "I'd better go to her."

"Sit down! Detective Inspector Wilkes is with her. Let's go through your movements."

"But we're not suspects, surely?"

"You stir things up and I would like to know just what you've been stirring."

John took over. "We decided to get out of the village. We

took a picnic and had that in the Green Park. We went round the shops, window-gazing. Then we stopped at that service station on the A40 and had an all-day breakfast."

"When?"

"About an hour and a half ago."

"You weren't up in New Cross trying to play detective?"

"No," said John, praying that the vicar would keep silent.

"So you went off together for the day. Why?"

"We wanted to look at the shops. That's all." John desperately improvised. "As a matter of fact, we took a walk around Kensington as well to see if there was a location that might suit us."

"What location? Why?"

John took a deep breath. He was tired and the news of this second murder had rattled him. "Because we're thinking of getting married."

Cursing him inside, Agatha forced a cheesy smile onto her face and said, "I didn't tell you before. I wanted it to be a surprise."

"And when is this wedding to take place?"

"We haven't fixed the date yet," said Agatha. "But when the time comes, Bill, I hope you'll give me away."

Bill's almond-shaped eyes fixed on both their faces. "I don't believe this," he said flatly. "But we will check out your alibi."

The questions continued. Had anyone talked to them in the shops, in Green Park, at Kensington? They were both tired and began to find it easy to lie, both sticking to their stories until Agatha almost began to believe they really were going to get married.

When the questions had finished, Agatha asked, "So does that mean Mr. Bloxby is in the clear?"

"No one is in the clear," said Bill. "Don't take any more trips in the next few days."

When they had gone, John could see that Agatha was about to round on him about their supposed forthcoming marriage.

"Save it," he snapped. "We've got to get on the phone to that vicar and to Mrs. Hill and tell them to keep quiet."

"You do it, O future husband of mine," said Agatha. "I'm going to get a drink."

"Get a large whisky for me at the same time. Before you do that, give me Mrs. Hill's number. I saw you taking a note of it."

Agatha gave him the number. She went into the sitting-room and poured a large gin and tonic for herself and a whisky for John and then sat down, hearing his voice talking on the phone, but unable to make out the words because she had closed the sitting-room door. They should have told Bill the truth, she thought wearily. It looked as if John had been right and that the murderer was down here in the Cotswolds.

The doorbell rang. She peered through the curtains and saw several members of the press outside.

She let the doorbell ring and sat sipping her drink until John joined her.

"That the press outside?" he asked.

"Yes, lots of them. Why on earth did you say we were getting married?"

"On impulse. This second murder rattled me. We can go along with it for the moment and then say we broke up."

"Bill didn't believe us."

"He will. All we have to do is look a bit lover-like when he calls again—which he will. Feel up to it?"

"I don't feel up to anything at the moment," said Agatha. "Why was Miss Jellop murdered?"

57

"She obviously knew something. I think the best thing for us to do is lie low and let things quieten down. We can go and see Mrs. Bloxby when the coast is clear. She'll know all about Miss Jellop. Who were the two others Mrs. Bloxby talked about?"

"Peggy Slither over at Ancombe and Colonel Tremp's widow."

"We can't very well talk to them with police and press swarming all over the place. Do you want me to stay the night?"

"No," said Agatha. "I thought we had sorted all that out."

"I only meant for protection. Someone might want to shut you up as well."

Agatha gave a shudder but said, "I'll be all right."

The phone rang. "You get it," said Agatha.

John went out to the phone in the hall and then returned a few moments later. "Press," he said. "I thought your number was ex-directory."

"It is, but the press have ways of finding out ex-directory numbers. Unplug it from the wall as you go."

"Meaning you want to be alone?"

"Exactly."

John took a gulp of the whisky in his glass, placed the glass carefully on the table and made for the door.

"Scream if you want me," he called.

Agatha sat nursing her drink after he had left. From time to time the doorbell shrilled. The press were persistent. They must have seen the police car outside her cottage earlier.

Then she rose stiffly and went up to bed. She carefully removed her make-up and peered at her face in the magnifying mirror in the bathroom. The lines around her mouth seemed to have got deeper. She undressed, took a quick shower, pulled on a night-dress and crawled into bed and lay staring up at the beams in the ceiling. At last the shrilling of the doorbell fell silent and she sank into an uneasy sleep.

It was early afternoon the next day when she remembered the phone was still unplugged and reconnected it. She dialled John's number. "What are you doing?" she asked.

"Writing. But I've got something for you. I'll be right over."

"Knock the door, then, don't ring and I'll know it's you."

Agatha was wearing an old blue linen dress and flat sandals. She wondered whether to change into something more fashionable, but then reminded herself—it was only John.

When the knock came at the door, she answered it. John followed her through to the kitchen and put a small jeweller's box on the table. "I think you'd better start wearing that to keep up the fiction."

Agatha opened the box and found herself looking down at an engagement ring, a large sapphire surrounded by diamond chips.

"When did you get this?" she asked.

"Years ago. It's my ex-wife's. She flung it in my face just before we broke up. Try it on."

Agatha slid it on over the wedding band she still wore. It was a perfect fit.

A tear rolled down her face and plopped on the kitchen table.

"What's up?" said John.

Agatha gave a shaky laugh. "I still have the engagement ring James gave me. I couldn't bear to wear it although I still wear his wedding ring."

John gave her a brief hug. "Best you wear a different one. Unless I'm mistaken, Bill Wong will be back soon. I'll make us some coffee. Those cats of yours are prancing all over the kitchen table. Do you allow that?"

"I'm afraid I let them do what they like. The table's scrubbed regularly. Still, you're right." She lifted both cats off the table, opened the door to the garden and shooed them out.

John was spooning coffee into the percolator when the doorbell rang.

"I wonder if that's the press again." Agatha went to the front door and peered through the spy-hole. "It's Mrs. Bloxby," she called.

She swung open the door. "Come in. Poor you. What a nightmare. Where is your husband?"

"Helping the police with their inquiries."

Mrs. Bloxby sat down at the kitchen table. "Coffee?" asked John. "It'll be ready in a moment."

"Yes, please," said Mrs. Bloxby. "Milk and no sugar."

"Why Miss Jellop?"

"I just don't know," said Mrs. Bloxby. She accepted a cup of coffee from John. "Such a silly, harmless woman."

"Where did she come from? Everyone in Cotswold villages these days seems to come from outside. No wonder the locals complain about the villages losing their character."

"Miss Jellop moved here from somewhere in Staffordshire. I believe she was comfortably off. Her family were in jam. Jellop's Jams and Jellies. Not much known around here but very popular in the north."

"Does Alf have an alibi?"

"They don't know the exact time of death, sometime in the evening. Alf was working in his study and I remembered that Miss Jellop had phoned in the morning. She wanted me to call round because she said she wanted to talk to me about something. She was always complaining about happenings in the parish and she wanted the church livened up, as she put it.

Wanted to hire a steel band from Birmingham to perform at the services, that sort of thing. I phoned back late afternoon and said I would be around about nine in the evening. The door of her house was slightly open. There was no answer when I rang the doorbell and I went in, worried that she might have met with an accident." Mrs. Bloxby raised a trembling hand to her mouth. "And there she was."

"Did she have anything around her neck?"

"I couldn't see. I mean, I forced myself to check her pulse and then I phoned for the police and ambulance. But I couldn't bear to look at her closely."

"Villages are getting like the city," said John. "Nobody notices things the way they would have done in the old days, when everyone minded everyone else's business. There's a high hedge on either side of her garden, as I remember, that effectively screens the door from the neighbours on either side."

"Let's see," said Agatha. "She lived in a terraced cottage on Dover Rise up behind the general stores. It's a cul-de-sac. Surely someone must have seen someone walking along."

"If you remember, there are only four cottages in that row. Mr. and Mrs. Witherspoon were away in Evesham visiting their daughter. That's the first cottage you come to. Then there's Mr. and Mrs. Partington. They were in their back parlour away from the road for a good part of the evening watching a couple of rented videos and eating TV dinners. Then comes Miss Jellop, and at the end of the row, Miss Debenham, who was with her sister in Cheltenham and stayed there the night."

"How come you're so well-informed?" asked Agatha.

"I've had police in the vicarage half the night and they often talk as if I'm not there."

"So we come back to Miss Jellop," said John. "Did you overhear the police say anything about Tristan's bank account?"

"Yes, I did, as a matter of fact. He paid several sums into

his account over the past few weeks, but all in cash. Before this murder, they interviewed several of the women they think he might have preyed on, but they all swear they gave him nothing. They say they had been thinking about it. They even checked old Mrs. Feathers's bank account, but the only large sum—large sum to her—she had drawn out recently was to supply you with dinner, Mrs. Raisin. She evidently said he had promised to invest money for her, but women like Mrs. Feathers are frightened of old age and harvest every penny. The fact that Tristan even got her to pay for his meals says a lot for his charm."

"So did you hear how much he had in his account?" asked Agatha.

Mrs. Bloxby shook her head. Her usually mild grey eyes were full of worry and pain. "I am so worried about poor Alf. Did you find out anything?"

"We don't want the police to know," cautioned Agatha, "because they would give us a rocket for interfering." She told Mrs. Bloxby about the visit to New Cross and to Binser.

"If only it would turn out to be someone from London," sighed the vicar's wife. "The atmosphere in the village is poisonous, all these silly women telling the police that Alf was jealous of Mr. Delon."

Pale sunlight shining in through the kitchen window sparkled on the ring on Agatha's finger.

"That's a new ring," exclaimed Mrs. Bloxby.

"John got rattled and told Bill Wong we were engaged to cover up what we were doing in London," said Agatha.

"Perhaps you should have told him the truth," said Mrs. Bloxby. "Anything to get the investigation away from poor Alf."

"I really don't think Mr. Bloxby has anything to worry about," said John soothingly. "In order to suspect him of the first murder, they would need to think you were lying to protect him and no one could believe that."

Agatha was about to point out waspishly that John *had* suggested to her Mrs. Bloxby might be lying, but with rare tact refrained from saying anything.

"I'd better get back," said Mrs. Bloxby, rising to her feet. "Alf might be back any time and I wouldn't want him to find the vicarage empty."

"Do you want us to come with you? Aren't the press pestering you?"

"They've gone, apart from a few local reporters."

Agatha saw Mrs. Bloxby out and returned to John. "Let's switch on television and look at the news," he said. "Something big must have happened to send them running off."

"Wait until the top of the hour," said Agatha. "It's twenty to three. It'll be sport on every channel."

She lit a cigarette. "That's a filthy habit," remarked John.

"I know," she sighed, "but one I love a lot."

"We'll just need to wait. Things'll be easier if the press have gone. We could leave it until tomorrow and then try to see what we can get out of this Peggy Slither. She's in Ancombe and the police won't be hanging around there. Did Mrs. Bloxby say where she lived?"

"I can't remember. Wait and I'll get the phone-book." Agatha went out and came back with the telephone directory.

As Agatha turned the pages, John said, "I remember. Shangri-la. That was the name of her place."

"That's right. Gnomes in the garden. I remember. Here it is. Doesn't give a street, just the name of the bloody house, as if the snobby cow lived in a manor. Well, Ancombe's a small place. Should be easy to find."

They turned over various bits and pieces of what they knew until Agatha noticed it was almost three o'clock. "Let's look at the television news now."

They went into Agatha's sitting-room and she switched on

the television set and selected the BBC *24-Hour News* programme.

The announcer said, "The Liberal Democrats, the Scottish Nationalists, and the Unionists have combined to table a motion of no confidence in the government following the revelations that the defence minister, Joseph Demerall, had been accepting large sums of money from Colonel Gadaffi."

"So that's it," said Agatha. "The press won't be interested in a village murder, or murders. At least we should get some peace."

"I think I'll go and get on with my writing," said John, getting to his feet. "I'll call for you in the morning, say around ten."

"All right," said Agatha, although she suddenly did not want to be left alone.

"See you."

Agatha wondered what to do. A pile of shiny new paperbacks she had bought in Evesham lay on the coffee-table. She picked up the first one. *Jerry's Mistake,* it was called. Agatha sighed as she skimmed the pages. She shouldn't have wasted her money. It was a chic-fic book, which meant it would be about thirty-something women in London. There would be one Cinderella character who would have a gay best friend and the best friend would die from AIDS in the penultimate chapter. The hero would have muscled legs and be bad-tempered. She tossed it aside. The next was the first Harry Potter book. Agatha had bought it out of curiosity. She settled down to read and became dimly aware an hour later that the doorbell was ringing. She looked through the spy-hole and saw Bill Wong. With feelings of guilt and reluctance she opened the door. He was alone.

"I think it's time you and I had a chat, Agatha."

"Come in and bring the thumbscrews with you. We'll sit in the garden. It doesn't look too cold."

"No, it's nice and fresh after that storm."

Agatha collected two mugs of coffee and carried them out into the garden. Hodge and Boswell climbed up on Bill. Hodge settled on his lap and Boswell draped himself around Bill's neck.

"Amazing how those cats like you," said Agatha.

"I'd like to concentrate on the matter in hand, however." Bill gently removed both cats and put them down on the grass. "Now, Agatha, I see you already have the ring. But why do I get the impression that the pair of you were lying to me?"

"Because you've got a nasty, suspicious policeman's mind. We are very much in love. No, I'll be honest with you. We get along together very well and neither of us wants to go into old age alone. So we decided to get hitched."

"If you say so. No word of James?"

"I may as well tell you. That lying bastard never returned to that monastery."

"He'll turn up again. With your luck, probably on your wedding day."

"Forget about him. Any ideas why Miss Jellop was murdered?"

"I think she might have found out something. I think that was why she phoned Mrs. Bloxby. And yet Mrs. Bloxby said Miss Jellop was always summoning her to make some complaint or another."

"Was she rich?"

"Very comfortably off."

"Anyone inherit?"

"She hadn't left a will. Her nearest relative was a sister who lives in Stoke-on-Trent."

"Tell me, Bill—anything funny in Tristan's bank account?"

"Large sums of money, not great—five hundred here, six hundred there, all deposited in cash. Total around fifteen thousand. Seems he invented that family trust. He was born Terence

Biles. Father was a post-office worker, mother a housewife. Both dead. Tristan changed his name by deed poll when he was seventeen. His parents were dead then. Nothing in his past. Good exam results at school. Studied divinity. Had the curacy of a church in Kensington for a few years. Nothing sinister there. Vicar said Tristan had declared he wanted to work in a rougher area. He seemed genuinely sorry to let him go.

"So, Agatha, you haven't been poking your nose in where you shouldn't?"

"No. I really have gone off the idea of detecting. I want to live a long and quiet life."

Bill stood up. "If you hadn't said that, I might actually have begun to believe you really were getting married. But you wanting a quiet life? Never! Just make sure if you do find anything that you tell me."

After he had gone, Agatha sat on in the garden, deep in thought. What had happened to that ten thousand? The police would not have asked the bank about it because they didn't know about it. Perhaps Tristan had asked for it in bits and pieces so as not to alert the income tax.

Agatha phoned Binser's office and asked to speak to him. She finally got through to his personal secretary, Miss Partle. "I really do wish you would leave him alone," said the secretary sharply. "He is very busy."

Agatha drew a deep breath. "Look, lady, just get off your bum and tell him that Agatha Raisin wishes to speak to him."

"Well, *really*."

Agatha waited and then Binser's voice came on the line. "What now?" he said. "I've told you all I know."

"It's just about that ten thousand pounds. How did you pay it?"

"Cash."

"Cash!" echoed Agatha. "That's odd."

"I know it's odd, but I think Tristan twisted my mind. He said he was setting up a special account with a bank in New Cross. He could get started right away if he didn't have to wait to get the cheque to clear."

"I know you didn't want anyone to know you had been conned. Still, I would have thought a man like you would have sued him to get the money back."

"He sent it back."

"What! You didn't say anything about that. When?"

"About a month after I had confronted him. The money was delivered downstairs in a large envelope, addressed to me."

"Was there any letter with the money? Perhaps he was hoping to resume the friendship."

"No, there was no letter. I heard from him a week after that when he threatened to blackmail me. And as I told you, I said I would report him to the police if he did, and heard no more from him. Now, if you don't mind, Mrs. Raisin, as far as I am concerned the matter is closed. I have heard on the news about the other murder in your village. Obviously the murderer is in your neck of the woods. Goodbye."

Agatha replaced the receiver and stood thinking hard. What would have made Tristan return that money? Mr. Lancing, his vicar? No, it would have been more like Tristan to fake penitence and claim to have returned the money while keeping it.

She reached out to the phone again, meaning to call John and discuss this with him, but changed her mind. Tomorrow morning would be time enough. She didn't want to fall into the trap of needing John's company.

But when she lay awake in bed that night, she felt frightened at the thought that there was some unknown murderer out there. And a thatched cottage was the last place you wanted to try to get to sleep in when you were scared. Things rustled in the thatch overhead and the beams creaked. She decided, just before she fell asleep, that she would forget about the whole thing, see the police in the morning and ask permission to go abroad. She would stay in some foreign country, far away from danger.

In the morning, however, after two cups of black coffee and three cigarettes for breakfast, Agatha felt strong again. The fears of the night had gone. At ten o'clock, she heard the beep of John's car horn outside, locked up the cottage and went to join him.

As they drove to Ancombe, she told him about the visit from Bill and her phone call to Binser and the surprising news of the return of the money.

"There's something that man isn't telling us," said John. "Tristan wouldn't return the money like that. He must have threatened him."

"I dunno. There's something very straightforward about him."

"If he's all that straightforward, then why did he give us the impression that Tristan kept the money?"

"He didn't lie about it."

"Only by omission. Here's Ancombe. Look for a twee cottage."

"Nothing in the main street that I can see. Stop at the post office there and I'll ask."

John waited until Agatha returned with the news that Peggy Slither lived at the far end of the village in Sheep Street.

"There must be hundreds of Sheep Streets in the Cotswolds," said John, letting in the clutch and moving off.

At the end of the village, he turned right into Sheep Street.

"Only a few houses here. Oh, that must be it up ahead on the right."

Shangri-la was a modern bungalow. The front garden was bright with flowers and plaster gnomes. They parked outside and then made their way up a crazy-paving path to the front door. The doormat bore the legend GO AWAY. No doubt Peggy found it humorous. John pressed the bell and they waited while it rang out the chimes of Big Ben. "Is she Mrs. or Miss?" asked John.

"Don't know."

The door was opened by a dark-haired middle-aged woman. She had a sallow skin and the sort of twinkling humorous eyes of people who do not have much of a sense of humour at all.

Agatha introduced herself and John.

"Oh, the snoops of Carsely," she said in a husky voice. "I was just about to make a cup of tea. Come in."

The living-room was full of knick-knacks and plants. Beside the window, a palm tree grew out of an old toilet. One wall was covered in those tin advertising signs that antique dealers love to fake. On the other side of the window from the palm tree was a copy of the boy of Bruges, peeing into a stone basin. The three-piece suite was upholstered in slippery green silk and decorated with gold fringe.

"I'll get the tea," said Peggy.

John looked at the stone boy of Bruges. "I wonder how the water circulates?" he said.

"Awful thing to have in your living room," said Agatha. "Makes me want to pee myself."

"Do you think she is really trying to be funny with all this kitsch?" whispered John.

"No, I have a feeling she really likes it. Shhh! Here she comes."

Peggy entered carrying a tray. The teapot was in the shape of a squat fat man. The spout was his penis. Agatha suddenly decided she did not want tea. When Peggy handed her a cup, she placed it on a side-table.

"All this murder is quite exciting," said Peggy.

"Exciting?" Agatha looked at her in surprise. "I thought you were very fond of Tristan."

"Oh, we all were, dear. Such a gorgeous young man."

"When's the funeral?" asked John. "I forgot to ask."

"Some cousin's having the body taken to London for cremation."

"I would like to attend that funeral," said Agatha. "Do you know when it's going to be?"

"I don't think anyone will know until the body is released by the police. Of course, you had a thing with him, didn't you?"

"If you mean an affair," said Agatha stiffly, "I most certainly did not."

"But Mrs. Feathers is telling everyone she peered round the kitchen door and saw him kissing you good night."

"It was a social peck, that's all," said Agatha, becoming angry. "I thought you were close to him."

"Not close. He amused me. And women of our decaying ages, Agatha, do like to be seen around with beautiful young men."

"I do not need beautiful young men. I am engaged to John, here."

"Really?" Peggy surveyed John from top to bottom before turning back to Agatha. "How did you manage that?"

John said quickly, "Did you give Tristan any money?"

"Not a penny. Not that the poor lamb didn't try. Cost him a good few dinners before he gave up on me."

I hate you, thought Agatha.

"Where were you on the night he died?" asked John.

"Silly man. You're not the police, so I'm not even bothering to answer you. I thought it would be funny to see how you two snoops went about your business, but I'm beginning to find the whole thing rather boring."

Agatha stood up. Rage was making her intuitive faculties work overtime. "It's a good act you're putting on, Peggy, *dear*. But you were in love with him and somehow he suckered you and I'm going to find out how. Oh, by the way, did you know he was gay? Come along, John."

Peggy sat staring after them as they made their exit.

"That last remark of yours hit the old bag hard," said John when they were back in the car. "How did you guess all that casual jeering was a front?"

"Tristan, it turns out, was a complete rat and a blackmailer," said Agatha. "But he was glorious and charming. He made me feel fascinating and desirable. That was why he was so dangerous. People who have been conned by him—and to be honest, I could have been—will pretend he had no effect on them. But I can't imagine any woman being unaffected by Tristan."

"Except Mrs. Bloxby," said John. "Let's go and see Mrs. Tremp."

# FIVE

†

MRS. Tremp lived in a converted barn outside the village. Agatha remembered seeing her at various village events. She was a small, mousy woman, and when the colonel was alive, the locals reported that he bullied her.

They bumped down the pot-holed drive leading to her home. As they got out of the car, Agatha slammed the door, and rooks, roosting in a nearby lightning-blasted tree, swirled up to the heavens, cawing in alarm. The harvest was in, and the large field beside the house was full of pheasant pecking among the golden stubble.

The converted barn looked large and solid. Agatha rang the bell and they waited. The rooks came swirling back to their tree and stared down at Agatha and John with beady eyes. Agatha shivered. "I don't like rooks. Birds of ill omen."

"You mean ravens," said John.

The door opened and Mrs. Tremp stood there, blinking myopically up at them in the sunlight.

"It's Mrs. Raisin and Mr. Armitage, is it not?"

"Yes," said Agatha. "May we come in? We want to talk about Tristan Delon."

"Oh dear. I was just making jam . . . and . . . I suppose you'd better." She turned and walked indoors and they followed her into a huge sitting-room with long French windows. The furnishings were a comfortable mixture of old and new. The air was redolent with the smell of plum jam.

"Do sit down," said Mrs. Tremp. "I hope you don't mind, I keep the windows closed when I am making jam or I get plagued by wasps. What do you want to know about Mr. Delon?"

"We heard you were friendly with him," said Agatha.

"Yes, I was, and I was most distressed to hear of his death. And now this other terrible murder. There was never anything like this before you arrived in our village, Mrs. Raisin."

"Nothing to do with me. I don't go around murdering people. But I'd like to know who is for Mr. Bloxby's sake."

"He has only himself to blame for being a suspect," said Mrs. Tremp. "He was so jealous of Mr. Delon."

"I suppose Tristan told you that."

"He did let slip that he was having a difficult time with the vicar, yes."

"Did you know that he was gay?" asked John. "And that he tried to get women to give him money?"

She raised a gnarled and veined hand up to her suddenly trembling mouth. "I don't believe it. That's a wicked thing to say."

"I'm afraid it's true," said Agatha. "Did he try to get you to give him money?"

"He did tell me he had this project to start a club for the youth of the village. He said he would need help. I did offer to support him. In fact, I had a cheque ready for him. But he was killed, so he could not collect it. But I am sure he really did want to start this club. You must be mistaken. He was a real Christian."

"Mrs. Tremp," said Agatha firmly, "you are very lucky that he never collected that cheque. He would have pocketed the money. How much was the cheque for?"

"Five thousand pounds."

"That's a lot of money."

"I can afford it. My dear George left me very comfortably off. He did not like me spending money. I made all our jam and cakes and bread. He insisted on it. And he would go over my housekeeping books every week, and goodness me, he would get so angry if he thought I had spent a penny too much. We lived in that poky little cottage on the Ancombe road for years. So full of junk I could hardly move! He never threw anything away. I craved space and light. The cottage was so dark. When he died, I rented a skip and threw everything out and then I bought this place."

She gave a little smile. "Nice, isn't it?"

"How did your husband die?" asked John.

"In a fit of temper. I was always saying, do watch your blood pressure. I'm afraid it was the cigarettes that did it."

"He smoked too much?" Agatha thought guiltily of the packet of cigarettes in her handbag.

"No. What happened was I suddenly craved cigarettes. He wouldn't let me smoke. There was a new cut-price grocery shop in Evesham. I realized if I shopped there instead of the village shop, I could enter the village-shop prices in the housekeeping book, but save enough for a packet of cigarettes. He had said he was going for a round of golf. I had just lit one up when he came crashing in. He had forgotten something. He started to rant and rave about my smoking and then he made some strange gargling sounds and dropped dead."

She gave another little smile. "I sat down and watched him for quite a while before I phoned the ambulance. He was quiet for the first time."

"To get back to Tristan," said Agatha, "how did he first get in touch with you?"

"He called on me. He said he was doing the rounds for the vicar. He was so charming. He loved this house. He said he could live here forever. He said Alf Bloxby was a bully. I said I knew all about bullying and told him about my life with George."

"Alf Bloxby is not a bully," said Agatha firmly. "You have known him a long time. Can you see Mrs. Bloxby putting up with a bully?"

"Mr. Delon said she was very long-suffering. I think you have been listening to malicious gossip, Mrs. Raisin. Even if he were gay, where's the shame in that?"

"None whatsoever, except it was a fact he kept from the women he was tricking out of their money."

A mulish looked firmed Mrs. Tremp's normally weak features. "I think you had both better go. I am not going to listen to any more slander and lies."

She rose and went and held open the front door. "And don't come round here again."

"I think she deliberately smoked that cigarette to make her husband have an apoplexy," said Agatha waspishly. "Terrifying woman."

"There's one thing that came out of it," said John.

"What?"

"She said she had a cheque ready for him. If he was prepared to take cheques rather than cash, then our Tristan planned to get as much as he could and then disappear."

"Maybe. But if he'd taken village people's money and disappeared, he would need to leave the church, and it was his position as a churchman that made it easier for him to get money out of people."

"But if he had received some sort of threat on his life, he might have planned to leave the country."

"Humph," said Agatha, annoyed that she had not thought of any of that. "We've not got much. What do we do now?"

"It's early yet. We could go back up to London to try whatever church it was in Kensington that Tristan used to work at."

"Bill didn't say what church it was."

"We could ask around."

"It might be in west Kensington. Might take us all day."

"I'm willing to bet it's somewhere around south Ken," said John. "Our Tristan would want somewhere fashionable."

"What if the police call round again?"

"Well, maybe we'll leave it until tomorrow. Let's find out how Mrs. Bloxby is getting along."

Mrs. Bloxby led them through to the vicarage garden. "Alf is lying down," she said. "This has all been a nightmare."

They sat down in the garden. "And no word of anyone seeing a stranger in the village?" asked Agatha.

"Nothing at all. It's television, you see. So many people appear to have been indoors, glued to their sets. I often wonder what it was Miss Jellop wanted to talk to me about. Was it something important, or just one of her usual complaints?" Mrs. Bloxby sighed. "Well, I'll never know now."

"What about the press?" asked Agatha. "Some of them must have still been around. People might remember someone with a camera and think, oh it's just another one of them and not bother saying anything to the police. By the way, Tristan started off at a church in Kensington. Any idea which one?"

"It might be in the letter that Mr. Lancing wrote to Alf to introduce Tristan. Wait here and I'll look."

When Mrs. Bloxby went inside, John said, "We've been neglecting our local pub. That must be a hotbed of gossip at the moment. We'd better try there after we've finished with Mrs. Bloxby and get some lunch at the same time."

Mrs. Bloxby came back holding a letter. She held it out to John, much to Agatha's irritation. Agatha pushed her chair up next to John and they both read it at the same time. It described Tristan's need to move to the country for his mental health. It then said in the last paragraph that he had previously worked at St. David's in south Kensington before moving to New Cross.

"We'll go there tomorrow," said John. "It's probably someone from Tristan's past."

"I think poor Miss Jellop was very much from Tristan's present," pointed out Mrs. Bloxby.

"But she might have found out something," John persisted.

"Has that sister arrived?" asked Agatha. "Miss Jellop's sister? The one from Stoke-on-Trent?"

"I haven't heard anything," said Mrs. Bloxby. "If I do, I'll let you know."

"We're going to the pub for lunch," said Agatha. "Care to join us?"

"No, Alf will be up and about soon."

John and Agatha left her and drove the short distance to the pub. "We're getting lazy," commented Agatha. "I used to walk everywhere." This was not true, but Agatha only remembered her rare bursts of exercise. She even had a bicycle rusting in the shed at the bottom of her garden that she had not taken out for over a year. She remembered cycling with Roy Silver, her one-time assistant in the days when she had her own company. Strange, she thought, that he hasn't phoned. He must have read about the murders in the newspapers. And what of Sir Charles Fraith, her one-time friend and "Watson"? She gave a little shiver. Her friends were deserting her. Even Bill Wong looked at her with a policeman's eyes these days rather than with the eyes of a friend.

The pub was noisy and full of smoke, not from cigarettes but from the open fire. The landlord, John Fletcher, was bending over it, coughing and spluttering. "It's that last load of wood," he said when he saw them. "Green." He lit a fire-lighter and threw it in among the logs. Reluctant flames started to lick up round the wood. "That should do it." He straightened up, wiping his hands on his trousers. "Now, what can I get you?"

They both ordered beer and sandwiches and retreated to a table in the corner by a window, propped open to let out the smoke. The fire crackled, a comforting sound. Outside the open window and beyond the small car-park, golden fields of stubble stretched out under a pale sun. The air coming in through the window held the chill of autumn. If only these murders hadn't happened, thought Agatha, forgetting how bored she had been recently, it would be nice to sit here and eat sandwiches and drink beer and then go home and play with the cats.

John brought over their beer and sandwiches. "So what's the gossip?" asked Agatha.

"Nothing much," said the landlord. "At first they all thought the vicar did it, but there's been talk that our curate wasn't really a very nice person, and so people think it was someone outside the village."

A customer at the bar shouted that he wanted a drink and John left.

Agatha took a sip of her beer and made a face. She preferred gin and tonic but often ordered beer, knowing she wouldn't finish her half pint or want another. Alcohol was just about the most ageing thing a middle-aged woman could take.

There was the brisk tap of high heels on the stone-flagged floor to herald the arrival of Miss Simms, secretary of the ladies' society.

She was clutching a glass of rum and vodka. "Mind if I join you?"

"Please do," said John Armitage.

Miss Simms sat down on a chair next to Agatha. "Terrible about Miss Jellop, innit? But she had it coming to her."

"How's that?" asked Agatha.

"Always complaining and poking her nose into things. Terrible gossip, she was. You should have heard the things she said about you, Mrs. Raisin."

"I don't want to know," snapped Agatha. "Do you still think Tristan was a saint?"

"No, he did a nasty thing."

"What?"

"I met him in the village on the day before he was murdered. He asked me out. Said he was tired of all those old women in the village. Now, that wasn't a nice thing to say, but at the time, like, I was so flattered that he wanted my company because he asked me out for dinner."

"But that was for the evening I had dinner with him!" exclaimed Agatha.

"I know. I'm coming to that. I was to meet him in that new restaurant, Stavros, in Chipping Norton, at eight o'clock. By ten past eight, I'd ordered a drink. He still didn't show. By eight-thirty, I decided to leave. Well, I'd had a look at the menu and I knew I couldn't afford their prices, so I just paid for the drink, picked myself up some fish and chips in Sheep Street and went home. I phoned and Mrs. Feathers said he was entertaining you and couldn't be disturbed. When did he invite you?"

"The day before he was murdered."

"But he asked me out for dinner in the afternoon of that day," wailed Miss Simms. "I just don't understand it."

"Maybe he did it deliberately," said John. "He'd already made a dinner date with Agatha here. Maybe he enjoyed the thought of you sitting, waiting."

"But he seemed so nice, ever so nice, but now there's some murmurs that he could be a bit, well, cruel, like."

"Got any examples?" asked Agatha.

"Well, Mrs. Brown, her what comes with the mobile library, she said he was charming to her one week and then, the next, he announced in front of the other customers that the selection of books was for morons and some moron must have chosen them. Mrs. Brown chooses most of the books herself, everyone knows that. There was a bit of a shocked silence, but he stood there, looking so gorgeous and smiling so sweetly, that everyone sort of decided they must have misheard. Then old Mr. Crinsted near me at the council houses, Tristan used to call round and play chess with him. Mr. Crinsted said he was so glad of the company that he let Tristan win the first couple of times, but on the third, he beat him and he said Tristan got very angry and accused him of cheating."

"There's one good thing about stories like that going round the village," said Agatha: "people can't be thinking Alf Bloxby murdered Tristan in a fit of jealousy."

"No, not anymore. But then, people do say things like— but who else could have done it?"

"What about Miss Jellop?" asked John. "What's being said about her?"

"She wasn't very popular. Always complaining. I mean, she irritated people. But I can't see anyone wanting to murder her. Of course, people are saying she was being spiteful about the vicar, saying he murdered Tristan, things like that."

And what that amounts to, thought Agatha wearily, is that people will still be thinking of Alf Bloxby as a murderer. I must do something. But what? Just keep on ferreting around and hope I find something out.

Miss Simms finished her drink and left. "What should we do now?" asked Agatha.

"I don't know. We'll try that church in London tomorrow. In the meantime, let's go down to the library and look up the name 'Jellop' in the Stoke-on-Trent directory. We might get the sister's number and we could call her. Tristan obviously told Miss Jellop something that made her dangerous."

"Nothing here," said Agatha, half an hour later. "Not in the residential addresses."

"Jellop's Jams and Jellies. Try under the business addresses," said John.

Agatha searched the book. "Got it," she said.

"Write it down and we'll go back and phone in comfort."

Back at Agatha's cottage, she said, "Who's going to phone? You or me?"

"I'll do it."

Agatha went into the kitchen and petted her cats and let them out in the garden. She stood for a moment surveying the scene in front of her, and thinking the garden looked rather dull. Not having green fingers herself, she had hired a gardener, but he turned out to be expensive and lazy, so she had fired him and replaced the flowers with shrubs. Next year, she thought, she would start all over again and have a colourful display of flowers.

John came out to join her. "Miss Jellop's sister is a Mrs. Essex. A nice woman in personnel even gave me her home address. You want to try it?"

"No, you do it."

John gave her a surprised look, but went back indoors.

Agatha was suddenly tired of the whole business. She should leave it to the police. She wanted something else to occupy her mind. Anything else. She could not, somehow, relax in John's company. Agatha could not understand that it was John's regular good looks which fazed her. Such men were usually interested in prettier and younger women. Such men were not for the likes of Agatha Raisin. And Agatha was old-fashioned in that she could only relate to men when there was a sexual undercurrent.

When John returned again, he said, "I spoke to the husband. Mrs. Essex is down here, at Mircester police headquarters. Let's go. We might catch her as she comes out."

"We might not recognize her," said Agatha, reluctant to move.

"With luck, there'll be some sort of family resemblance."

"She might have left Mircester and be up at the cottage."

"I doubt it. I took a walk up there early this morning. It's still taped off and the forensic people are still working on it. Come on, Agatha!"

They waited in the car-park outside Mircester police headquarters, studying all the people coming out. After an hour, Agatha yawned and then shifted restlessly. "No one who even looks like her. I say we should go home. She probably left ages ago."

"That might be her," said John. A middle-aged woman had just emerged accompanied by a policewoman. She had protruding eyes and a ferrety appearance. A police car drove up and both women got in the back.

"Now what?" said Agatha.

"We follow them. She might be staying somewhere locally."

John, who was driving, followed the police car at a safe

distance. "They're going in the Carsely direction," said John after a few miles. "Maybe the police have finished with the cottage and she's going to stay there."

"Must be tough if she is," retorted Agatha. "I don't know that I'd want to stay in a house where my sister had been murdered."

"Maybe keeping an eye on her assets. She'll probably inherit."

Sure enough, the police car drove on down into Carsely.

"We'd best go home," said John, "and wait, and then walk up later when we're sure the police have gone. We'll go to my place."

Agatha always experienced a pang of loss when she entered John's cottage. There was no feel, no trace of her missing ex-husband's personality. James Lacey's books had spilled from the shelves. John's books were all in neat order, according to subject. He worked at a metal computer desk placed in front of the window. There were two armchairs covered in bright chintz and an oak coffee-table, shining and bare.

"Like a drink?" asked John.

"Gin and tonic."

"I don't have lemon or ice."

"How British! I'll drink it warm."

While John went into the kitchen, Agatha sat down and closed her eyes, trying to conjure up an image of James and of the room as it used to be. She had nearly succeeded when John came back in. She opened her eyes and accepted a glass of gin and tonic. He carefully put two coasters down on the coffee-table.

"You live like a bachelor," commented Agatha. "Neatness everywhere."

"It's the only way I can live. If I let it go for one day, then sloppiness sets in. There's a police car just gone past." He went to the door and opened it and looked out. "Bill!" he shouted. "In here."

"I feel guilty every time I look at him," grumbled Agatha.

Bill came in. He was on his own. "Was that you following us from Mircester?" he asked.

"We just happened to be in Mircester doing some shopping," said Agatha defensively. "We saw the police car in front of us. I didn't know you were in it."

"I wasn't. I was in the car behind you."

"Anyway, now you're here, what can we do for you?"

Bill studied Agatha's face and noticed the way she dropped her eyes and reached for her drink.

"I think you pair have been up to something. I've never known you to let things alone before, Agatha."

"It's this engagement," said John. "We've got so much to deal with. We don't know whether to keep one of our cottages or buy somewhere bigger."

"So you say. Have you heard anything?"

"Only that the villagers have been sharing views about Tristan and seem to be coming to the conclusion that he was rather nasty."

"Give me an example."

Agatha told him about Miss Simms. "Now, that *is* odd," said Bill. "I mean, what would a gay man want with a woman without money?"

"Probably did it out of spite."

"It still seems out of character. If he was out to fleece rich women, then he would be anxious to keep up his front of being sweet and charming. He must have known that Miss Simms would talk about it."

"Unless," said Agatha slowly, "someone or something frightened him and he'd decided to leave. That was why he wanted the church money. He probably hoped to get a cheque from me."

"Or he decided to dump Miss Simms because you provided a possibility of good pickings."

"But he asked Miss Simms out for dinner after he'd invited me. Did Miss Feathers say if he had received any calls during the night?"

"Not that she knows of, apart from the one from you."

"Miss Simms must have been very flustered and excited about that invitation," said Bill. "I wonder if she got the evening wrong. You had dinner with him on the Tuesday. I wonder if he said tomorrow evening and in her excitement, Miss Simms misunderstood him."

"I'll phone up the restaurant and see when he made the booking for," said John.

"You'll need an Oxfordshire phone-book," said Agatha.

"I've got one. You two go on talking; I'll phone from the bedroom."

"So you're really going to get married again," said Bill, scrutinizing Agatha's face.

"Seems like a good idea."

"Women of your age often marry because they want companionship, or someone to go into pubs and restaurants with, or to mend fuses; but not you, Agatha."

"I've decided I'll never fall in love again," said Agatha. "So I may as well settle for companionship. Can we talk about something else? Like is Miss Jellop's sister going to stay in her cottage?"

"How did you know it was Miss Jellop's sister?"

"The police car turned off in the direction of Dover Rise. Simple."

"Now, why do I get the feeling that the pair of you found

out that she was at police headquarters and waited outside and tailed her back here?"

"Because you've got a nasty, suspicious copper's mind. Oh, here's John."

"Mystery solved," said John, coming down the stairs. "Tristan booked a table for the Friday evening, not Thursday. The restaurant was quiet, so when Miss Simms turned up, saying she was waiting for a gentleman friend, but not giving any name, they put her at a table for two."

"Another dead end," said Bill. "I'd best be off. Don't go bothering Mrs. Essex."

"Who's she?" asked Agatha innocently.

"As if you didn't know!"

When Bill had left, John asked, "Are we going to bother Mrs. Essex?"

"Of course," said Agatha.

"Better leave it a bit until we're sure the police have gone. That's Mrs. Bloxby just gone past the window. She's probably on her way to your place."

He opened the window and called, "Mrs. Bloxby!" She turned and smiled and then walked up to the door. John opened it and ushered her in. Mrs. Bloxby was looking so relaxed and cheerful that Agatha cried, "You look great. You must have heard some good news."

"I haven't heard any good news. But I've been in church and I have renewed my faith."

Agatha felt embarrassed. She said, "Bill Wong has just been here." She told the vicar's wife about Miss Simms's date, ending up with, "But I don't see why he even asked her in the first place."

"I think," said Mrs. Bloxby slowly, "that perhaps he was not gay."

"But by all accounts he said so himself," exclaimed Agatha.

"He may have said that as one of his ways of rejecting and hurting people. Men who are very beautiful are naturally assumed to be gay. I must confess I made that mistake myself. Think, Mrs. Raisin, when you had dinner with him, did you ever think he might be gay?"

"No, I didn't," said Agatha. "He was exuding sexual vibes."

"If he was as cruel as he seems to have been, it might have delighted him to lead both men and women on. To the men, he could imply he was gay and then reject them if they made any advances. To the women, he could say he was gay, and reject them that way. He liked manipulating people. He did at first imply that I was wasted on Alf, but, you see, that didn't work with me, for I have never fallen out of love with my husband."

Agatha felt a sour pang of jealousy which she quickly dismissed. Mrs. Bloxby deserved the rewards of a good woman. Maybe I should pray myself, thought Agatha.

They all went over what they knew about Tristan without getting any further.

When Mrs. Bloxby had left, John glanced at his wristwatch. "Perhaps we should try Mrs. Essex now."

They walked up through the village to Dover Rise. "If she was well off," said John, "it's a wonder she didn't choose somewhere a bit more expensive to live. I think these used to be workers' cottages at one time."

"She was on her own and probably didn't feel she needed anywhere larger. One of these terraced cottages costs nearly two hundred thousand pounds. Living in the Cotswolds is expensive. Everyone wants to live here. A lot of people who had second homes in the Cotswolds during the last recession opted to sell their London homes and commute from here. It's only an hour and a half on the train from Moreton. If you live in Hampstead, say, it can take you all that just to get into the City."

They stood at the end of the cul-de-sac and looked along it. "No police cars," said John. "I can't see a copper on duty either."

"Why are they called coppers?" asked Agatha.

"It comes from an old acronym, COP, constable on patrol. Why are you playing Trivial Pursuits, Agatha?"

"Because I'm nervous. I expect Bill Wong to leap out of the bushes at me."

"Looks all-clear."

"I hate this business of being unauthorized," Agatha burst out. "We look like a couple of Nosy Parkers."

"The curse of the amateur detective," remarked John cheerfully. "Buck up, Agatha. Where's your stiff upper lip?"

"To quote the Goons, it's over my loose wobbly lower one."

They arrived at the cottage. The door was standing open. "Here goes!" said Agatha.

She rang the bell beside the door, suddenly aware that she was wearing trousers, a shirt blouse and flat sandals. I'm letting my appearance slip, thought Agatha. I haven't been to the beautician in ages. I hope to God I'm not growing a moustache. She nervously felt her upper lip. Was that a hair? She fumbled in her handbag and took out a powder compact and peered in the little mirror.

"Yes? Can I help you?"

Agatha lowered the compact and found Mrs. Essex staring curiously at her.

Agatha tucked the compact hurriedly in her handbag. She introduced both of them as friends of Miss Jellop and said they had come to offer their condolences.

"Too kind," said Mrs. Essex. Her protruding eyes stared at Agatha's face with such intensity that Agatha wondered if she was, after all, sprouting a moustache.

"We would like to talk to you about your sister," said Agatha.

"Why?"

Agatha took a deep breath. Where had all her old confidence gone? "I have helped the police on murder cases before," she said. "I thought we might be able to help find out who murdered your sister if we could ask you a few questions."

"But I have already told the police all I know!"

John edged in front of Agatha. He gave Mrs. Essex a charming smile. "As you may know, I write detective stories."

"What's your name again?"

"John Armitage."

Her pale lips parted in a smile. "Why, I saw you on the *South Bank Show* last year. Please come in. This is exciting."

Hardly the grieving sister, thought Agatha sourly as she followed John into the cottage.

"I'm just making an inventory of everything," said Mrs. Essex. "Poor Ruby never spent much on herself."

Ruby, thought Agatha. So that was her first name. Momentarily distracted, she began to wonder about the first names of other women in the ladies' society where the tradition was to use second names.

Then she realized John was speaking. "Your sister phoned Mrs. Bloxby, the vicar's wife, asking her to call round as she had something to tell her, but by the time Mrs. Bloxby got here, your sister was dead. Did Miss Jellop say anything at all to you that might indicate she knew something dangerous about someone?"

"No, because we didn't speak. We had a falling-out. I was amazed when the police told me they had found Ruby's will and that she had left everything to me. In fact, she had changed her will the day before she died."

Agatha's bearlike eyes gleamed. "Who had she left her money to in the previous will?"

"To that curate. The one who was murdered. Poor Ruby. She was always getting these schoolgirl crushes on some man or another."

"And you didn't know anything about it?" asked Agatha.

Those protruding eyes fastened on Agatha's face with a flash of malicious intelligence. "Meaning did I murder my sister the minute I knew she'd changed her will? You should leave detecting to your friend here."

"Might there be something among her papers?" put in John quickly. "Letters or diary or something?"

"You'll need to ask the police. They took all her papers away. Now, if you'll excuse me, I have a lot to do."

"Will you sell the cottage?" asked Agatha.

"I don't know. Maybe keep it for holidays and weekends. My husband's due to retire soon."

"When did you last speak to your sister?" asked Agatha.

"Must have been about three years ago."

"Not much there," said John gloomily as they walked back down through the village. "You know, the car has caused a decline in gossip in English villages. I suppose not so long ago one would see people standing gossiping and walking about. Now a lot of them even use their cars to drive a few yards to the village stores."

"But that means empty roads and lanes," said Agatha impatiently. "Surely a stranger would have been noticed. Unless it was someone masquerading as a local reporter. The village is fed up with the press. They see someone that looks like a journalist and they shy away. I can tell a genuine journalist a mile off."

"How?"

"Even if they're well-dressed, they carry a shabby sort of people-pleasing alcoholism about with them."

"You're sour because you were a public relations officer."

"You're right," said Agatha reluctantly. "I hated crawling to the bastards."

"I can't imagine you crawling," said John. "I can imagine you frightening them into writing what you wanted them to write."

This was in fact true but Agatha didn't want to hear it or believe it. She still saw herself as a waiflike creature—shy, vulnerable and much put-upon. Sometimes when she looked in a full-length mirror, she could not believe that the stocky, well-groomed woman looking back at her was really herself.

They walked on in silence and then Agatha said, "What next?"

"Just keep on trying. London tomorrow."

# SIX

†

"YOU look very nice," commented John when Agatha got into his car the next morning. Agatha was wearing a silky gold jersey suit. It had a short skirt. Her best feature, her legs, were encased in sheer tights and her feet in high-heeled sandals.

"Thanks," said Agatha gruffly. She had decided it was time she started dressing up again, not, she told herself, that this sudden desire to smarten her appearance had anything to do with John Armitage. She wished she had elected to drive them herself. There was something about John doing all the driving that was making her feel diminished. Agatha liked to feel in charge at all times. Subconsciously she had felt that putting on her best clothes might prompt some sexual interest in her from John, and in that way, she would have the upper hand. But what Agatha's subconscious decided hardly ever reached the conscious part of her brain.

"Look at that dreadful advertisement," exclaimed John, driving along the M40.

"What? Where?"

"We passed it. It said, 'Only ninety-one shopping days to Christmas.' "

"The shops are full of Christmas crackers and wrapping already," said Agatha. "The adults have ruined Christmas for the children with all this commercialism."

"Wrong. The children have ruined Christmas for the adults."

Agatha looked at him, puzzled. "How do you explain that?"

"They've come to expect to get exactly what they want. I know all this from friends of mine with children. Something new comes out in July, say. They clamour for it. No use saying, 'Wait till Christmas.' They have to have it right away because it'll be old hat by Christmas. They don't want surprises. They want what they demand. So there are no shining faces under the Christmas tree, radiant with surprise and gratitude. Only complaints like, 'Why did you buy me this computer game? It's *months* old.' Greedy children and disappointed parents, that's Christmas."

"But surely it's the parents' fault. Can't they put their foot down and say, 'You'll get what we give you and nothing costing more than five pounds'?"

"And never, ever be forgiven? It's the kids these days who have to keep up with the Joneses. They don't want to go back to school after the holidays and be unable to compete with the others. I'm going away for Christmas."

"Where?"

"Don't know. Stick a pin in the map."

"I'll probably go away somewhere myself, but only for a short time. I don't like leaving my cats."

"Your cats seem to adore Doris Simpson."

"They're my cats!"

"Possessive, aren't you? We may as well think of going somewhere together."

"Why?"

"Well, why not? Unless you prefer to go places on your own."

"Actually, I like my own company when I'm travelling."

"Suit yourself. I'll find someone else. Look at that idiot in front, veering from lane to lane like a maniac."

I should grow up, mourned Agatha. It would have been nice to have company. Why did I get miffed because he didn't say anything affectionate? Why should he? Why should I want him to?

She ruthlessly shifted her mind onto the problems of the Carsely murders. Why had John decided that Tristan was gay? Jealousy? Agatha thought back to that dinner. She had largely blotted it out of her mind because of that final rejection. No, he had not struck her as gay. She was sure he masqueraded as one to lead women on and then rebuff them. Perhaps he had lured men on and then told them he was heterosexual. It could be that he had behaved himself while at the church in South Ken. Could he have been twisted and spoilt by his exceptional looks? Hardly. There must have been something twisted in him from the beginning.

How did those journalists that she had been so bitchy about cope with day-to-day rejections and dead ends? Perhaps she should have been nicer to them during her career as a public relations officer. Perhaps, had she done so, she might have been even more successful.

Agatha hardly ever questioned her own behaviour, but this rare introspection was caused by a longing to forget about the whole case. She felt obscurely that it was because John kept taking over. He didn't have to suffer from the same setbacks as she did. People mostly recognized his name and were prepared to speak to him. And because he was a man, she thought sourly. Men investigated. Women were regarded as interfering. Had women's lib all been a myth? All that seemed to have been achieved was that women were expected to work as well as raise families. Respect for women had gone.

She roused herself from her meditations to realize they were approaching south Kensington and John was saying, "Look out for a free parking meter." They cruised around until they struck it lucky. A man was just moving his car out from a parking meter two streets away from the church.

"I hope it turns out to be someone from Tristan's past in London," said Agatha. "I want Carsely to go back to being its old time-warp-dull sort of place."

"I might agree with you," said John, "had it not been for the murder of Miss Jellop. I hope we can find someone at the church. With all the thefts these days, a lot of these churches stay locked up."

Agatha looked at her watch. "It's getting on for lunch-time. Some of them have a lunch-time service."

St. David's was a small Victorian church tucked in between two blocks of flats. To Agatha's relief, the door was standing open.

She followed John in, noticing with irritation that John as usual was leading the way. The church was dark and smelt of incense. Agatha looked at the burning candles and at the Stations of the Cross. "Isn't this a Catholic church?" she asked.

"No, Church of England. Very High. All bells and smells."

A man in shirt-sleeves came out of a side door and approached the altar. "Excuse me," called John.

He approached them down the aisle. He was wearing a grey shirt and black trousers. He had a thin intelligent face.

John introduced them and explained why they were anxious to find out all they could about Tristan.

"I am Hugh Beresford," he said. "I am the vicar here."

"And were you here when Tristan was curate?" asked Agatha.

"Yes. I was distressed to read about his murder. So sad."

"What was his behaviour like when he was here?"

"Exemplary, until . . ."

"Until what?" demanded Agatha sharply.

"I should not speak ill of the dead, although it was not entirely his fault."

"You'd better tell us," said John. "We're desperate for any morsel which might help us find out what happened to him." At that moment a woman entered the church, sat in a back pew and then knelt down in prayer. "Is there anywhere private we can talk?"

"Yes, follow me."

He led them up the aisle and through a heavy oak door at the left of the altar, down a stone passage where surplices hung on hooks, and through another door into a small wood-panelled room furnished with a plain desk and chairs. "Please sit down," said the vicar. "I will tell you what I know, but I really don't think it has much bearing on the case. I feel I should really not be telling you anything I have not said to the police, but as you explained, your local vicar is in danger of being falsely accused and so I suppose I should do everything to help. Now where shall I begin?"

The room was dark and stuffy. Agatha could hear the muted roar of the traffic on the Old Brompton Road. The chair she was sitting on was hard and pinched her thighs. She was getting pins and needles in one foot and eased her bottom from side to side.

"Tristan was a very charming young man. At first, he seemed a great asset to the parish. But I suppose having such good looks could only lead to trouble. Before I go on, you must assure me that everything I tell you is in confidence."

"Absolutely," said Agatha and John nodded.

"Right. A very attractive lady started attending the services. She started to get friendly with Tristan. Of course, other ladies in the congregation became jealous and one told me that Tristan was having an affair with this lady. I challenged him. He said they were going to be married. Now this lady was a divorcée in her late forties. I pointed out the age difference and the difference in circumstances."

"Such as?" asked Agatha.

"She was very wealthy and high-class. I told Tristan he would be damned as a toy-boy. But he would not listen. I thought of reporting the matter to the bishop, but I kept putting it off. He was so very much in love, you see."

Agatha raised her eyebrows. "Tristan? In love?"

"Possibly I should not have done what I did, but I called on this lady. The minute I explained the difficulties there would be for her in marrying someone so young she burst out laughing and said Tristan was a dear boy and very amusing but she had no intention of marrying him. I said if that was the case, she should leave him alone. She was raising hopes in him that could not be fulfilled."

He fell silent. Did Tristan really love this woman? wondered Agatha. Or was he dazzled with the thought of wealth and a sophisticated life?

The vicar took up the story again.

"In telling him that all was off and that she had no intention of marrying him, she let fall that I had been to see her. Tristan came back in a rage and accused me of ruining his life. He said he was sick of being poor."

"So he wasn't really in love with her," exclaimed Agatha. "It *was* her money he was after."

"Dear me," said the vicar. "I never thought of it like that. Before it all came to an end, he was . . . glowing."

"And who was this woman?" asked John.

"I really do not think I should tell you. She has moved from this parish anyway."

"We really will be discreet," said John. "We are neither journalists nor the police."

Again the vicar fell silent.

At last he said, "It was Lady Charlotte Bellinge."

"And do you know where she is now?" asked Agatha.

"I am afraid I do not."

They thanked him and made their way out of the church. "So how do we find this Charlotte Bellinge?" asked John.

"I've got friends in newspapers who could look up the files, but they would want to interview us about the murders. I know—*Gossip* magazine. I know the social editor. We'll try her."

Tanya Cartwright, the social editor of *Gossip,* quailed when she learned that a Miss Agatha Raisin wanted to see her. Agatha had once done public relations for a businessman who wanted to break into London's social scene. Tanya had caved in and had written him up in her column just to get rid of the terrifying Agatha Raisin. "Tell her I'm out," she was saying to her secretary just as the door of her office opened and Agatha and John walked in.

"Some woman's bothering me," she said brightly. "How

nice to see you, Agatha." She dismissed her secretary with a wave of her hand. "Take a seat."

John was amused. Tanya was a brittle, thin woman with a hard face, which her latest face-lift had done nothing to soften. Her eyes were disconcertingly huge. Gold bracelets dangled from one bony wrist. But she looked terrified of Agatha.

Agatha introduced John and Tanya relaxed a fraction. "So pleased to meet you," she said. "We must do a profile on you sometime."

"Delighted," said John. "May I explain why we're here?"

"I'll explain," said Agatha harshly. She outlined the tale of the murders and then asked if Tanya knew where Charlotte Bellinge could be found. Relief that Agatha was not going to badger her to put some social-climbing nobody into her column flooded Tanya's face. She switched on her computer. "Wait a bit. I should have an address here. She gets mentioned in the social columns quite a lot." She moved the mouse and clicked. "Let me see. Yes, here she is. Number Twenty-five Parrot Street. It's off the King's Road in Chelsea."

"I know where it is," said Agatha. "Thanks a lot, Tanya. We'd best be off."

They had just left Tanya's office when the social editor opened her door and cooed, "A word with you, Mr. Armitage."

John went back in and Tanya closed the door firmly, leaving Agatha on the outside.

John emerged after only a few moments. "What was that about?" demanded Agatha.

"She just wanted to meet me for lunch sometime."

"Oh," grunted Agatha. "She might have asked me."

"She's not attracted to you," said John with a certain air of smugness.

They had left the car in an underground car-park. "Better

leave it where it is," said John. "I don't want to have to drive around Chelsea looking for a parking place. We'll take the tube to Sloane Square and walk along."

The King's Road in Chelsea always reminded Agatha of her youth, when she was struggling to claw her way up the business ladder. That had been during the days when a good address mattered and she had paid an expensive rent for a flat in Draycott Gardens and had very little money left over for anything else. In the evenings, the restaurants had been crammed with trendy young people, laughing and drinking, and Agatha, on the outside looking in, would feel intensely lonely, with only her ambition to keep her warm.

She shrugged off her memories as they turned the corner of Parrot Street. Charlotte Bellinge lived in a thin white-stuccoed house. "At least someone's at home," she remarked. "One of the downstairs windows is open."

John rang the bell and they waited. The door swung open and a young girl stood there. She had a pale spotty face, a stud in her nose and five little silver earrings in each ear. She was wearing a short tube-top exposing a pierced belly-button.

"What?" she asked.

"Is Lady Bellinge at home?" asked Agatha.

"Who wants her?"

"Here's my card," said John, stepping in front of Agatha. The girl disappeared, only to reappear a few moments later to say, "Come in."

She opened the door to a sitting-room on the ground floor and Charlotte Bellinge came forward to meet them. She was exquisite: small, dainty, perfectly groomed. Her face was un-lined and her large eyes were of an intense blue. Her hair was tinted a pale shade of gold. She was wearing a loose white silk shirt and tight black trousers.

"Now, why is a famous detective writer calling on me?" she asked.

Agatha and John sat down and John explained the reason for their visit while Agatha felt sulkily that she was been pushed to the sidelines, again.

"But how fascinating!" drawled Charlotte when John had finished. "Quite like one of your detective stories. I don't see how I can help you. Tristan was a gorgeous boy and yes, he did have a crush on me."

"Did you have an affair?" demanded Agatha, not liking the way John was staring at Charlotte with a dazed smile on his face.

"No, I did not. But he amused me and he was so very beautiful. He did, however, become demanding. I am not made of money."

"He asked you for money?" Agatha leaned forward.

"Not in so many words. But when I took him out to some smart restaurant, he would complain his clothes were too shabby, so I paid to have him tailored and all that." She waved one perfectly manicured little hand. "But then he began to ask for things as if he had some sort of right. So I got bored and said he ought to be going around with people of his own age and to leave me alone. He made some feeble attempt to black-mail me, threatening to tell the social columns that I had been having an affair with a curate. I told him if he did, I would sue him. I wanted to move to Chelsea anyway, so I moved and was glad to get away from him. He had become . . . quite frighten-ing. I think he lived in fantasies. I think he believed I would actually marry him and he would live in the lap of luxury. He did crave the good life. I remember once when we were in a shop, he was looking at a cashmere sweater and he kept stroking it like a lover. He begged me to buy it for him and became so shrill that I did, to avoid a scene."

"Were you surprised when you learned he was murdered?" asked Agatha.

"Yes, very surprised. If I had learned that Tristan had murdered someone, I would not have been nearly so surprised. So boring, all this raking over the past." She turned a dazzling smile on John. "Do tell me about your books."

And so John did and at great length, while Agatha shifted restlessly. When he had finally finished, Charlotte looked curiously at Agatha. "Are you two an item?"

Agatha opened her mouth to say they were engaged, but John said quickly, "We're only pretending to be. You see, we didn't want the police to know we had been up in London finding out things, so I invented the lie we were engaged to divert their suspicions."

Charlotte gave a tinkling laugh. "How funny! You are very amusing, John." She picked up her handbag, opened it and extracted a card. "My mobile-phone number and e-mail address are there. We should meet up for dinner one evening."

"That would be wonderful," said John.

"Excuse *me,*" snapped Agatha. "*If* we could get back to the matter in hand: Did Tristan court any other women in the parish that you knew of?"

"No." The beautiful eyes drifted back to John. "He seemed totally wrapped up in me."

"Hardly surprising," commented John. They gazed at each other and Agatha could have slapped them both.

She stood up, stocky and militant. "We'd best be going, *dear.*"

"What? Oh, yes, of course."

"Sophie will show you out."

"Your daughter?" asked Agatha.

Charlotte let out a trill of laughter. "No, my maid. They

don't wear caps and aprons like they did in your day, Mrs. Raisin."

Agatha led the way. John hung back. She heard him saying, "I'll phone you soon," and then the amused murmur of Charlotte's voice, "Next time leave your dragon behind."

"She could have done it, mark my words," said a truculent Agatha as she stomped her way along the King's Road.

"Nonsense, Agatha. She wouldn't hurt a fly. But we know one thing. Tristan was just the same sort of person in London as he was in New Cross."

"I suppose so," conceded Agatha, suddenly not wanting to appear jealous. "Where do we go from here?"

"Back to Carsely. I feel we let Peggy Slither's nastiness put us off. Perhaps if I saw her on her own . . . ?"

"By all means, try," said Agatha, thinking that John in Carsely was at least not John entertaining Charlotte Bellinge in London. "But there's one thing we've been forgetting. Who attacked Tristan in New Cross? Were the police called in? I wish we could ask them."

"We could try that vicar, Lancing, again. I mean, he didn't tell us at first about Binser, so he may be holding back other information."

"Okay," said Agatha, "back to New Cross."

"I really don't think you should keep coming round here," said Mr. Lancing an hour later, when they were once more seated in his study. "I have told you all I know."

"The thing that puzzles us," said Agatha, "is this business about the attack on Tristan. Was it reported to the police?"

"No, it was not. Tristan became almost hysterical. He had to go to hospital and he told them there that he had suffered a bad fall. He kept saying over and over again that he wanted to get away. He seemed truly repentant about that business with Binser."

"Did you know he had returned the money?" pursued Agatha.

"Yes, because he assured me he had."

Agatha gave a click of annoyance. "You didn't tell us that. You let us assume he had not."

"I am afraid that after he had left, and on calmer reflection, I came to the conclusion that he had not. Now you tell me he did return the money, which relieves my conscience. He must indeed have been truly repentant."

"I doubt it," said John. "I don't think repentance was in his nature. I'm beginning to think the return of the money and the beating were connected. I think we should have another word with Mr. Binser."

But this time there was no audience with the businessman. His formidable secretary, Miss Partle, received them instead. She said that Mr. Binser was abroad on business but that he would no longer be available to answer their questions. "He has done enough, considering you have no official status," said Miss Partle. "But as a matter of interest, what brought you back here?"

John tried delicately to put the case of the beatings and the return of the money while Agatha studied Miss Partle. She was typical of an executive secretary. Plain, middle-aged, sensibly dressed with intelligent eyes behind thick glasses. Those eyes were surveying John with increasing contempt. When he had finished, she said, "I think you should keep fiction for your books, Mr. Armitage. We are not the Mafia. We do not hire people to beat anyone who annoys us. We believe in dealing with the law. And talking about the law, do the police know that you are investigating?"

"I have helped the police in the past," said Agatha defensively.

"Meaning that in this case, they do not know, and I think they should be told. Please do not trouble us again."

On the road home, Agatha and John anxiously debated whether Miss Partle would actually tell the police. By the time John turned the car into Lilac Lane, they had come to the comfortable conclusion that she would not. Neither she nor Binser would want his friendship with Tristan exposed.

And then they saw the police car outside Agatha's cottage.

They drew up and Wilkes and Bill Wong got out of the car. "Probably something else," John reassured Agatha. But Agatha reflected uneasily that it had taken them nearly three hours to get back because of an accident on the M40—time enough for Miss Partle to have consulted her boss and then phoned the police.

Wilkes looked grim. "I think we should talk about this inside," he said.

Agatha opened her cottage door and led the way into the kitchen with her cats at her heels. She opened the kitchen door and let them out into the garden.

"Now," she said with false brightness, "what can I do for you? Would you like a coffee, or maybe something stronger?"

"Sit down," commanded Wilkes. "We have just had a certain Mr. Binser's lawyers on the phone. Mr. Binser is making a statement which they are faxing over. As you evidently already know, he was conned out of ten thousand pounds by Delon, money which was returned. He told you this and hoped that would be the end of it because he said being tricked in such a way might bring his business judgement into disrepute. He says that as the murder took place here and had nothing to do with him, he did not feel obliged to contact us before this. He says the reason he is doing so now is that you both had the temerity to suggest to his secretary that he had hired people to beat Delon up. What all this amounts to is that you have been withholding valuable information and interfering in a police investigation. I should charge you both and arrest you.

"But I will admit you have been a little help to us in the past, Mrs. Raisin, so I will tell you this. You are not to conduct any more investigations into this case."

"If we had not found out about Binser," said Agatha crossly, "then you wouldn't either."

"Perhaps. But as far as I can judge, Binser has nothing to do with the case. He is a very powerful man with powerful friends in high places and I would like to keep my job until it is time for me to retire. Do not approach him again, do you understand me?"

"Yes," said Agatha meekly.

"So what else have you found out? What else have you been keeping to yourselves?"

Agatha was about to say, "Nothing," but John told them all about Charlotte Bellinge. "I know she's got nothing to do with this," he said, "but we thought if we could get a better picture of what Tristan was really like, we could maybe discover the type of person who would kill him."

"Miss Jellop's connections were all in Stoke," said Bill, speaking for the first time. "I cannot see that she could have anything to do with such as Mr. Binser or Charlotte Bellinge. All you have done is to tread on the toes of the rich and powerful, Agatha, and, incidentally, lie to me about it."

Agatha turned red.

"You will both come with us now to police headquarters," said Wilkes, "and make full statements, and I mean full statements, and then I hope you will both get on with your respective lives and leave policing to the police."

"And that's that," said Agatha, three hours later when they emerged from Mircester police headquarters. "It's one in the morning and I'm starving."

"There's an all-night place on the Mircester bypass," said John. "Let's go there and go over what we've got."

"Don't see much point in going on," said Agatha. "And you'd better have your ring back."

"Not right away. I think it would be the last straw for Bill if he knew we had been lying to him about that as well."

The all-night restaurant was a depressing place, redolent with the smell of old grease. They collected plates of sausage, egg and chips and sat down at a window, their tired faces lit by the harsh fluorescent lighting.

"It lets Binser out," said John.

"I suppose it does," agreed Agatha. "All we did was goad him into going to the police, and if he had anything to hide and had previously used criminal means to hide it, he wouldn't have opened up to the law. Damn! I should have trusted my first judgement. I thought he was a nice man and honest and one that was only furious that he'd been so taken in by Tristan."

"Which brings us straight back to the Cotswolds," said John. "You know, that rudeness of Peggy Slither could have been to keep us away. I'll try her tomorrow and you can see if you can get anything more out of Mrs. Tremp."

"And what if they phone the police?" said Agatha miserably.

"Well, maybe not tomorrow. Tell you what, I'll get on with my writing and you get on with whatever it is you usually get on with and we'll let the police settle down."

Agatha slept late the next day and awoke feeling still tired and still guilty about having lied to Bill. She phoned John to see if he would like to join her for dinner that evening but he said he had just checked his contract and he was going to be late delivering his latest book if he didn't get down to it. "So I'll need to leave real-life murder for a bit. See you around. In fact, I've got to go up to London to see my agent and publishers tomorrow and I may stay there for a few days. All right if I leave my keys with you? Just in case there's a gas leak or something like that."

"Sure," said Agatha.

"I'll pop them through the letter-box tomorrow."

"I've got to go," said Agatha. "Someone at the door."

It was Mrs. Bloxby. "I heard you had the police round last night, Agatha. Anything up?"

"Come in. It's amazing. Someone bumps off Miss Jellop and nobody sees a thing, and yet you know I had the police here last night." Agatha told her about Binser's complaint.

Mrs. Bloxby sighed and sat down and placed her battered handbag on the kitchen table. Look at her, thought Agatha, mangy old handbag, droopy cardigan, baggy tweed skirt, and yet she always appears the picture of a lady. "If only you could find out who did these dreadful murders," said the vicar's wife. "Nothing in the village will ever be the same if you don't."

"I'm shackled at the moment," said Agatha. "The police will be furious if I carry on, and I think they'll charge me next time."

"Did you find out anything else?"

Agatha told her about Charlotte Bellinge. "Tristan must have been furious," said Mrs. Bloxby. "Beauty, titled lady, wealth, and all snatched from him."

"He thought he was using her and all the while she was just using him," said Agatha.

"So he was probably not gay although it is so hard to tell, with all of us being such a mixture of masculine and feminine."

"Anyway, it appears the London end is closed."

"I don't think that matters. Surely it is something to do with someone here."

"Tell me about Peggy Slither," said Agatha. "Is there a Mr. Slither?"

"She's divorced. Her husband, Harry, was a wealthy businessman. He was having an affair. She hired a private detective and when she'd gathered enough evidence, she sued him for divorce. She already had money of her own, but she took a lot from him, including the house. He had evidently once jeered at her over what he called her vulgar taste and the minute the house was hers, she redecorated—I think—in a way that would infuriate him."

"I think John is going to try her again on his own. Do you know her very well?"

"Only through charity work or when the Ancombe Ladies' Society and our own get together. She is not popular."

"She evidently was with Tristan."

"I don't think he really cared what women were like as long as they had money."

Ouch, thought Agatha, so much for my charms.

"But," continued the vicar's wife, "the parish work must go on. We need some event which will raise a good sum for Save the Children. We seem to have done everything in the past—jumble sales, whist drives, fêtes, country and western dances—there must be something else."

"People like to gamble," said Agatha.

"I thought of a fishing competition." Mrs. Bloxby opened her handbag and drew out a small yellow plastic duck with a hook in its head. "The scouts use these for fishing contests—you know, fishing lines and tanks of water and a prize for the person who hooks the most ducks."

"No money in it," said Agatha. She took the duck from

Mrs. Bloxby and examined it. "I've got an idea," she said. "If you took the hook off and weighted the duck underneath for balance and put a cocktail stick with a flag on the head instead of the hook, you could have duck races."

"Duck races?"

"Yes, you see, that would bring in the gambling element. We could ask Farmer Brent if we could use the stream on his land. We run, say, six races and get people to sponsor each race and get their name on it. John Fletcher at the Red Lion could sponsor a John Fletcher race, and so on. Have a refreshment tent. Have a gate with entrance fees. Planks laid across the stream for starting and finishing points. I'll be bookie and get them to place bets on the ducks. Small prizes for the winners. Take the ducks back at the end of each race, dry them out and sell them again for the next one."

"It could work," said Mrs. Bloxby. "We'd be awfully dependent on the weather."

"The long-range forecast says October is going to be a good month. Put posters up in all the villages."

"I'll get to work on it," said Mrs. Bloxby. "It will take my mind off things. You are a great loss to public relations, Mrs. Raisin."

"I'll talk to Farmer Brent and get his permission, I'll arrange the posters and publicity."

"Do you know what you mean to do next?" asked Mrs. Bloxby. "I mean, in finding out who committed these murders?"

"I'll keep digging around," said Agatha.

The next morning, Agatha found John's keys lying inside her front door. She picked them up and put them in the pocket of her slacks. Perhaps, she thought, Mrs. Essex might have discovered or remembered something. I might get more out of her on my own. After a breakfast of two cigarettes and two cups of black coffee, she fed her cats and then set out for Dover Rise.

As she was passing John's door, she noticed a package sticking out of his letter-box. Better pop it inside, thought Agatha. Like that, it's an invitation to thieves.

She fished out his keys, extracted the package, picked up letters from the floor and placed them all on his desk. The phone began to ring. She stood listening to it, wondering whether to answer it when it clicked over onto the answering machine. A voice said, "John, dear, this is Charlotte Bellinge. Looking forward to seeing you for dinner tonight. Would you be a dear and bring me a signed copy of one of your books? 'Bye."

Agatha sat down by the desk and twisted the bright engagement ring round and round on her finger. Of course John must be investigating further, she tried to tell herself. But then she thought of the beautiful and exquisite Charlotte and shook her head dismally. It was obvious John couldn't wait to see Charlotte again. And he hadn't told her.

Feeling very much on her own, she locked up and left and went to her own cottage. What of her former Watsons—Charles Fraith and Roy Silver? She would get one of them on the case with her and show John Armitage that she did not need him.

But when she phoned Roy's office, it was to be told he was working out of the New York office, and Charles Fraith's aunt informed her that Charles was in Paris.

Agatha stood up and squared her shoulders and set her mouth in a grim line. She would solve this case herself.

# SEVEN

†

AGATHA had decided that Mrs. Essex would have probably returned to the north before she arrived at the cottage, but Mrs. Essex herself answered the door.

"Oh, it's you," she said. "Come in. Maybe you can tell me what I should do with this lot. They're down in the cellar," she said, leading the way to a door under the stairs.

As Agatha bent her head to follow her through the low door and down shallow stone steps, she wondered if Mrs. Essex had found something gruesome.

"There they are," said Mrs. Essex.

The small cellar was full of metal wine racks stacked with dusty bottles.

"I wouldn't have thought your sister would be a wine collector," said Agatha.

"If you mean fine wines, forget it. This lot is all home-made. See!" She took a bottle out of the nearest rack. A faded white label with the inscription "Jellop's Brew" had been stuck on the greenish glass.

"Is it any good?" asked Agatha.

"I never touch alcohol, so I wouldn't know."

Agatha thought of the duck races. Nothing like a bit of alcohol to get the punters going. And home-made wine would not be considered sinful.

"If it tastes all right, I could maybe take the lot off you for a church fête."

"What! All of it?"

"Yes, how much would you want?"

"If it's for the church, you can have it. I could turn this cellar into a big kitchen. The one upstairs is like a cupboard. But you'd better try some first. We'll take this bottle upstairs and I'll find you a glass."

Agatha reflected it was a bit early in the day for alcohol. On the other hand, it was probably pretty mild.

She led the way upstairs and Mrs. Essex followed her carrying the bottle. The living-room smelt damp and musty. "Ruby was too mean to get central heating in," said Mrs. Essex, as if reading her thoughts. "Have a seat and I'll get a glass."

At least she's being friendly, thought Agatha. I might just find out something.

Mrs. Essex returned with a corkscrew and a glass. She drew the cork and poured Agatha a glass of golden liquid. Agatha sniffed it cautiously. Then she took a sip. It was sweet and she normally didn't like sweet wine, but it slid pleasantly down her throat and sent a warm glow coursing through her veins.

"So have you found out anything relevant to my sister's murder?" asked Mrs. Essex.

"No, nothing. All I can think of is that Tristan told her

something about somebody and that somebody found out she knew and decided to silence her. Would she keep such information to herself without telling the police?"

Agatha took another large gulp of the wine.

"If she did know something, she might not realize how important it was. She liked secrets and she liked power. Ruby wasn't a nice person. I know she's dead. But the fact is that she tormented the life out of me when we were growing up. I remember once . . ."

Her voice went on, describing the iniquities of Ruby while Agatha refilled her glass, enjoying the effect of the wine. It was as if all the golden warmth of summer were surging through her body.

She realized Mrs. Essex was asking her a question. "I beg your pardon," said Agatha dreamily.

"I was asking how you pass your time in this village. It seems so cut off."

"Oh, there's the ladies' society. We're always arranging events to raise money for charity."

"Forgive me, but you don't look the type to enjoy that sort of thing. Are you married?"

"I was."

"Where is he now?"

"I don't know," said Agatha. A dark tide of misery flooded her. She told Mrs. Essex all about James, all about how he had pretended to be taking holy orders while fat tears coursed down her cheeks. She went on to tell the bemused lady about her past, about her struggles, about her life, until she realized that somewhere in this sad tale, Mrs. Essex had gone into the kitchen, taking the remains of the bottle of wine and had replaced it with a steaming mug of coffee.

"Drink that," said Mrs. Essex. "You must forgive me for saying so, but you are drunk."

Shock sobered Agatha somewhat. "I'm sorry," she said. "I don't know what came over me."

"Alcohol's what came over you. It looks as if that stuff's pretty lethal. Do you still want it?"

"Oh, yes. I'll get John at the pub to collect it and we can stack it somewhere in the church hall. I'll ask Mrs. Bloxby where it should be stored." Agatha rose unsteadily to her feet. "I'll jusht be on my way."

Mrs. Essex scribbled something on a piece of paper and held it out. "That's my phone number. Give me a ring when they're coming to collect the wine."

Agatha looked at her helplessly. "Shorry."

"It's all right. I think you should go home and sleep it off."

Agatha was sure the fresh air would restore her, but she had to walk home very slowly and carefully as her legs were showing an alarming tendency to give way.

With a sigh of relief she opened her front door and went into the sitting-room. She would just lie down on the sofa until her head cleared.

When she awoke, the room was in darkness. Her cats were sitting on her stomach looking down at her, their eyes gleaming.

Agatha straightened up and they jumped down on the floor and headed for the kitchen, mewing crossly.

What time is it? wondered Agatha. She stumbled to the door and switched on the light and stared in amazement at her watch. Eight o'clock in the evening. She hurried into the kitchen and opened cans of cat food. Once the cats were fed, she made herself a cup of coffee and sat down at the kitchen table and lit a cigarette. With the first puff, memory came flooding back. With dreadful clarity she remembered telling Mrs. Essex everything about her life. Her face flooded with colour and she let out a groan. She wondered what proof that wine was. It had seemed such a good idea for the duck races. She picked up the phone in the kitchen and dialled the vicarage number. When Mrs. Bloxby answered, Agatha told her all about the wine. "It's heady stuff. Do you know I gave Mrs. Essex my life story after only a couple of glasses? Do you think it would be safe to serve it?"

"It's in a good cause," said the vicar's wife. "And she is giving it away. We'll sell it by the small glass and warn everyone it's very strong."

"I feel such a fool," wailed Agatha.

There was a long silence.

"Are you still there?" asked Agatha anxiously.

"Yes. I'm thinking. Something just struck me. If it loosened your tongue so effectively, it might have done the same to Tristan Delon's."

"So it might," said Agatha slowly. "I've never behaved like that before. He might have been blackmailing someone we don't know about. John was going to see Peggy Slither again, but he's gone off to London. I might try her myself. I'm going to phone John Fletcher and ask him if he can pick up the wine tomorrow. Where do you want it stored?"

"In the church hall. I'll leave it open tomorrow morning. We could really do with a proper church hall. That one is too small for events and we always have to use the school hall."

"Maybe the duck races could be used to raise money for a new one."

"Tempting. But Save the Children comes first."

"Okay. Can you think of any excuse I could use to talk to Peggy Slither again?"

Mrs. Bloxby sat in thought. Then she said, "We could involve the Ancombe lot in the duck races. Old Mrs. Green is the chairwoman of the Ancombe Ladies' Society, but she is poorly at the moment. Peggy is the secretary. You could call on her as my emissary and propose to her that we join forces."

"Excellent. I'll do that."

"I'll phone John Fletcher at the pub and ask him if he'll send the truck round to pick up the wine," said Mrs. Bloxby. "If the wine is as powerful as you say, perhaps we should mix it with fruit juice and serve a punch."

"Might be safer," conceded Agatha. "Tell John to call Mrs. Essex and tell her what time the truck will be there. I'll try Peggy Slither tomorrow. I'm still feeling shaky."

After Mrs. Bloxby rang off, Agatha put a frozen shepherd's pie in the microwave. It never struck her as odd that she should be prepared to spend time cooking for her cats and yet be content with microwave meals for herself.

Agatha had tried to get interested in cooking. The Sunday supplements for the newspapers were full of recipes and coloured photos of delicious meals. Everyone who was anyone knew how to cook exotic dishes these days.

But it was very hard to plan exotic meals for one. She poked at the microwaved mess on her plate, forcing herself to eat some of it so that she would not wake up hungry during the night.

It's just as well I'm not in love with John, she thought, as she finally settled down for the night. I wish him well with that tart, Charlotte Bellinge. But as if to give the lie to this thought, her cats sidled into the bedroom and leaped onto the bed, something they only did when they sensed she was upset.

Agatha drove reluctantly to Ancombe the next morning to face Peggy Slither. She now wished she had waited for John's return and sent him instead. After all, he was the one who had promised to go. She found herself hoping that Peggy was not at home. But as she parked, got out, and approached the garden gate of the bungalow, she saw Peggy stooped over a flower-bed.

"Hi!" said Agatha.

Peggy straightened up from her task of planting winter pansies and surveyed Agatha with disfavour. "Why do British people keep saying hi, as if they were Americans? I blame television."

"Oh, really. Well, a good day to you and how *do* you do," said Agatha acidly, forgetting that she had meant to be nice to Peggy and so encourage her to talk.

"So what do you want?" demanded Peggy.

Agatha outlined the idea for the duck races and Peggy visibly thawed. "I'll make the decision to join forces with Carsely," she said. "Mrs. Green should never have been made chairwoman. Come inside and let's discuss dates and arrangements."

Back into that horrible living-room. Agatha said that the twenty-third of October, a Saturday, would be a good day.

"What if it rains?" asked Peggy.

"I'll get a marquee set up in the field for refreshments. If it rains, the races will just need to take place all the same."

"Will Farmer Brent agree to let us hold it on his land?"

"I'll go and see him," said Agatha. "I only know him slightly. I was introduced to him in the pub. He seems a friendly sort. Mrs. Essex, Miss Jellop's sister, is contributing home-made wine."

"Is she living in her sister's house already?"

"She's just clearing up. I think she and her husband plan to use it for weekends."

"Must say it's pretty insensitive of her, her sister being recently murdered and all. I think the Jellop woman was slightly off her head."

"Did you know her?"

"Not very well. Sort of in the way I know the rest of you women from Carsely."

"Tristan knew her well. Did he talk about her?"

"Had a giggle with me about several of the old biddies in the parish. I can't remember him saying anything about her in particular. You detecting again?"

Agatha was suddenly sure that she was lying. She was sure that Tristan had said something about Miss Jellop.

"I'm curious," she said. "There's a murderer on the loose."

"You've done this sort of thing before, if I remember."

"Yes."

"Is this how you go about it? Ask questions? Any questions?"

"Something like that," said Agatha. "People sometimes remember things they haven't told the police."

"I could do that."

"Why should you?" demanded Agatha crossly.

"Because I'd probably be better at it than you." Peggy's eyes gleamed with a competitive light.

God, I really do *hate* this woman, thought Agatha.

"I have a lot of experience in these cases," said Agatha stiffly.

"Yes, but I knew Tristan very well."

"Not well enough to find out anything that might relate to his murder," said Agatha, hoping to goad her into some revelation.

"That's what you think. If you can find out things, so can I. I remember, you even got your picture in the newspapers a couple of times."

"I didn't do it for fame or glory. As a matter of fact, the police took the credit in nearly every case."

"So you say," jeered Peggy.

Agatha had had enough. She stood up. "The police don't like amateurs interfering in their investigation."

"Oh, really? So what about you? You have no professional status."

"I am discreet."

"Agatha Raisin discreet!" Peggy gave a great horse laugh and that braying laugh followed Agatha as she marched out of the door. She gave a fishing gnome a savage kick as she passed and it tumbled into a small pool.

"I'll show her," muttered Agatha as she got into her car. "But how? I'm at a dead end."

Once home again, she sat down at her computer and began to type out everything she had learned. As she typed, the engagement ring on her finger winked and flashed. She took it off and put it in the desk drawer.

The doorbell rang. She saved what she had typed and went to answer it.

Bill Wong said, "I think it's time we had a chat, Agatha."

"Come in," said Agatha reluctantly. "I'll make coffee."

"Instant will do."

Agatha switched on the kettle. Her cats jumped up on Bill, purring loudly. He patted them and then removed Hodge from his shoulder and Boswell from his knee and placed them gently on the floor.

Agatha made two cups of coffee and placed them on the table along with milk and sugar. "I think I've some cake left," she said.

"Never mind the cake. Sit down. I want to talk to you. I see you're not wearing your ring."

"I was typing on the computer and it kept flashing in the light and distracting me. What do you want to talk to me about?"

"I've never known you before to let things lie in a murder case," said Bill. "I feel damn sure you've been ferreting around. Is there anything you haven't been telling me?"

"You know about Binser. Yes, I've been asking a few questions but not getting anywhere. Someone Tristan knew, like Miss Jellop, learned something about the murderer."

"I should think that's pretty obvious."

"Unless it wasn't related. Unless maybe her sister bumped her off."

"Mrs. Essex has a cast-iron alibi. Now out with it. Who have you been talking to?"

"You may as well know. I went to see a Mrs. Peggy Slither this morning."

"Why her?"

"That repulsive woman was friendly with Tristan. But she won't tell me anything. The silly cow has decided to turn detective herself."

"I'd better see her. If she's holding anything back, she might tell me. Where does she live?"

Agatha gave him directions. Then she said, "There was Mrs. Tremp."

"We spoke to her. Apart from the fact she was about to give Tristan money and was saved by his murder is all we know. Think, Agatha. Has anyone else in this village got enough money to have attracted Tristan's attentions?"

"There are a good few around. I can't bring anyone to mind. I mean, sometimes in the Cotswolds, people with a good amount put by for their retirement live in quite modest homes. People are living so long these days and they all dread the inevitable high fees of a nursing home."

"I'll ask Mrs. Bloxby," said Bill. "She might be able to think of someone. Where's John Armitage?"

"He's up in London." Agatha coloured faintly. Had she told Bill about Charlotte Bellinge? Better keep some bits of the investigation to herself. Pride would not let her confess to Bill that John had gone up to London to see an attractive woman.

"There's a favour I want to ask you," said Bill. "You know I told you about my girl-friend, Alice."

"Oh, yes. That still on?"

"Very much so," said Bill, beaming.

"Been to meet your parents yet?"

"No."

Obviously not, thought Agatha, or it wouldn't still be on. "You see," continued Bill, "I feel I've made mistakes in the past by introducing my girl-friends to my parents too early on. Makes them think I'm getting too heavy. But I would like Alice to meet my friends. I've got the evening off. May I bring her over?"

"I'd be honoured," said Agatha. "Bring her for dinner."

"Maybe not. She's a vegan."

"Oh dear. But I think I can cope."

"No need to do that. What if I bring her for drinks, say, for an hour about seven o'clock and then I can take her for dinner somewhere."

"Right you are."


When Bill had left, Agatha returned to her computer and ran over what she had already written.

If Miss Jellop had learned something from Tristan, something dangerous, then it must be about someone in Carsely or one of the other nearby villages.

And what of Mrs. Tremp? Perhaps it would be a good idea to try that lady again. She decided to walk. Too much driving everywhere meant she wasn't getting enough exercise. But as she trudged up out of the village, she was assailed again by the old longing to just let herself go, stop chasing after men, give up the battle against age. John Armitage, whom she had almost come to think of as asexual, had fled off to London, apparently smitten by Charlotte Bellinge. There was a faint hope that he might be trying to find out something relevant to the case, but Agatha doubted it. And how could a stocky, middle-aged woman compete with a porcelain blonde? Not that I want to, thought Agatha. I mean, I'm not at all interested in John. I wonder if I should go blonde. Do blondes really have more fun? Why not try? She tugged her mobile phone out of her handbag and called her hairdresser. Yes, they had a cancellation and could fit her in at three that afternoon.

Mrs. Tremp was at home and not at all pleased to see Agatha. "If you've called to ask me about the murders, I don't know anything," she said.

"I actually called to see if you could help with the duck races," lied Angela.

Mrs. Tremp looked diverted. "Duck races? What on earth are they?"

Agatha explained.

"That does sound a good idea and I do like to help in charity work. Come in. What is it you would like me to do?"

"Last time I was here you said you were making jam," said Agatha. "I wondered if you would consider setting up a table at the races and selling some of your home-made jam? You need not contribute what you make for any sales to the charity if you do not want to. It's just that stands with home-made jams and cakes lend a country air to the proceedings."

"Oh, no, I'll be glad to contribute. Who is making the cakes?"

"I thought I might ask the members of the ladies' society."

"No need for that. Do sit down, Mrs. Raisin. I will bake cakes as well. To be honest, time does lie heavily on my hands. The colonel when he was alive kept me so busy. As a matter of fact, I've just made some carrot cake. Would you like some?"

"That would be very nice."

"Tea?"

"Yes, please."

When Mrs. Tremp retreated to the kitchen, Agatha wondered how to broach the subject of Tristan. Perhaps just talk about the races and village matters and see if Mrs. Tremp herself volunteered anything.

The carrot cake proved to be delicious. Agatha ate two large slices, comforting herself with the thought that the walk home might counteract the calories. She talked further about the plans for the races and then volunteered the information that Mrs. Essex was contributing a cellar-full of home-made wine.

"Who is this Mrs. Essex?" asked Mrs. Tremp.

"Miss Jellop's sister."

"How odd! She is staying at her sister's home?"

"Only, I think, to clear up. I believe she and her husband plan to use it for weekends and holidays."

"Sad, that. I mean, the life is draining out of the villages. I mean, the community life. Soon the whole of the Cotswolds will be some sort of theme park full of tourists, incomers and weekenders. There are few like you, Mrs. Raisin, who are prepared to do their bit. I am sorry I was so cross with you, but the murder of poor Tristan upset me. He had a way of making me feel good about myself. I suppose the secret is to feel good about oneself without relying on other people, but that is a very hard thing to do. Of course, I have wondered and wondered what could have brought about his death. He was extremely attractive. Perhaps it was a crime of passion."

"Could be. Somehow I think it was to do with money and somehow I get a feeling that after I left him on his last night something happened to make him want to run for it. Has anyone said anything about anyone strange being seen in the village?"

"I only usually speak to people in church or people in the general stores. They are all mystified."

"If you can think of anything, let me know." Agatha tactfully turned the conversation back to village matters and then took her leave.

When she returned home, she checked her supply of drinks to see if she had a good-enough selection, ate a hurried lunch of microwaved lasagne and got into her car and drove to the hairdresser's in Evesham, all the while telling herself that she did not really need to go blonde, she could always change her mind at the last minute.

Early that evening, she rushed up to the fright magnifying mirror in the bathroom for yet another look. Her thick hair was a warm honey-blonde . . . and yet . . . and yet . . . she did not feel like Agatha Raisin. Agatha went into the bedroom for a look in the wardrobe mirror. A stranger looked back at her. She was wearing a plain black georgette dress, cleverly cut to make her look slimmer than she was. Perhaps some eye-shadow? She went back to the bathroom. She carefully applied beige eye-shadow, then liner and mascara, and had just finished when the doorbell rang.

"You've gone blonde!" said Bill, goggling at her. "This is Alice."

"Come along in," said Agatha.

As she led the way to the sitting-room, she heard Alice mutter, "You said she was *old*."

And then Bill's quiet rejoinder, "I said older than me."

Agatha crossed to the drinks trolley. "What will you have, Alice?"

"Rum and Coke."

"Oh dear," said Agatha. "I don't know if I've got any Coke."

"Sherry will do, if you've got that," said Alice.

"I'll have a soft drink," said Bill.

"Tonic water?"

"That'll be fine."

Agatha busied herself with the drinks, handed them round, and sat down opposite Alice and Bill, who were seated side by side on the sofa. It was the first occasion since their arrival that Agatha was able to get a good look at Alice. She had curly brown hair, wide eyes and a pugnacious jaw. She had a generous bosom, a thick waist and chubby legs.

"Have you known Bill long?" asked Alice. She took Bill's hand in hers and held it firmly.

"Ever since I came down here. Bill was my first friend."

"Seems odd." Alice took a sip of her drink and wrinkled her nose. "I like sweet sherry," she said.

"I don't have any of that. May I offer you something else?"

"Don't bother. Just put this in a bigger glass and add some tonic water."

Oh dear, thought Agatha, but did as requested. "What's odd?" she asked.

"Well, I mean, Bill being young and you old."

"We were not having an affair," said Agatha acidly.

"Found out anything more about the case?" asked Bill hurriedly. Why, oh why, he wondered, did Agatha Raisin have to go blonde and put on a slinky dress?

Agatha shook her head. She told them about the duck races. Alice laughed, a harsh and brittle sound. "Kids' stuff."

I will not be nasty to this girl for Bill's sake, no matter what she says, vowed Agatha. "Oh, it will be amusing, I assure you," she said lightly. "How do you enjoy working in the bank, Alice?"

" 'Sawright."

"Interesting customers?"

"Some of them. Some of them think the bank's a bottomless pit of money. They come in saying the machine outside won't give them anything. I just tell them, 'You're wasting my time and your own. If that machine says you can't have any money, then you can't.' " She laughed. "You should see their faces."

How can Bill like such a creature? marvelled Agatha. But Bill was smiling at Alice fondly.

Alice stood up. "Can I use the little girls' room?"

"It's at the top of the stairs."

When Alice had left, Bill grinned. "I'm rather enjoying this."

"Why?" demanded Agatha.

"I've never seen Alice jealous before. You would choose this night to turn yourself into a blonde bombshell."

"I should find it flattering, but I'm finding this visit awkward, Bill. Are you really keen on her?"

"I think this is the one, Agatha. You're seeing her at her worst. You should be flattered."

Agatha opened her mouth to say she wasn't feeling flattered at all when Alice returned. Deciding to keep the conversation away from Alice, Agatha discussed the case with Bill while all the time she thought, he really mustn't get tied up with such a creature. But she promised herself she would not interfere in his life.

But as they were leaving, Agatha said politely, "Give my regards to your parents, Bill."

Alice, who had reached the front door ahead of Bill, swung round. "*I* haven't met your parents. *I* would like to meet your parents."

"And so you shall," said Bill. "Thanks for the drinks, Agatha. I'll call you soon."

Agatha slammed the door behind them. Bill's formidable mother would soon send Alice packing, but what a horror she was. Agatha surveyed herself in the hall mirror. She sighed. It just wouldn't do. Then she was struck by the thought that John, seeing her as a blonde, might get the idea that she was trying to compete with Charlotte and she would look pathetic. Agatha resolved to get it all dyed back the way it was as soon a possible.

She had arranged so that the phone would not ring during Bill's visit. She picked up the receiver to put it back on the ringing tone and found she had a message. She dialled 1-5-7-1 and waited. "You have one message," said the carefully elocuted voice of British Telecom. "To listen to your messages, please press one." Agatha did that and Peggy Slither's voice sounded, "I'm streets ahead of you. You'll never guess what I found out. I'm just going to check a few more facts and then I'm going to the police."

Agatha saved the message. I don't think she knows anything at all, she thought. She bit her lip. She picked up the receiver again and arranged the ringing tone and replaced it again. She was just turning away when it rang. It was Mrs. Bloxby. "How are things with you, Mrs. Raisin?"

"I'm not getting any further. Oh, Bill was just round with his latest love and she's horrible. Nasty bullying sort of girl."

"Well, as you've pointed out before, they never last after a visit to his parents."

"He hasn't taken her to see them yet but he's going to, so that should be the end of that."

"I gather from what you've told me that he usually favours nice quiet girls. Maybe this one will be a match for his mother."

"No one," said Agatha with feeling, "is a match for Bill's mother. Oh, there's something else." She told the vicar's wife about her visit to Peggy and the message she had just received.

There was a silence and then Mrs. Bloxby said, "I don't like this. I can't help remembering the time when Miss Jellop phoned me up. Do you think she could be in danger?"

"I don't know. She did know Tristan pretty well. I tell you

what, I'll phone her and see what she's up to. Probably just bragging. I'll let you know."

Agatha rang off and looked up Peggy's number in the phone-book and dialled. She got the engaged signal. She went into the kitchen and looked in the freezer for something to microwave. The cats wove their wave around her ankles. "You've been fed—twice," complained Agatha. She picked out a packet of frozen steak-and-kidney pudding and put it in the microwave to defrost. She tried Peggy's number again, but it was still engaged. She returned to the kitchen and heated the steak-and-kidney pudding and shovelled the mess onto a plate. The cats sniffed the air and then slunk off, uninterested. Agatha picked at her food with a fork. After she had managed to eat most of it, she dialled Peggy's number. Still engaged.

I'll drive along and see her, thought Agatha. She went upstairs and changed into a sweater, slacks and flat shoes. She tied a scarf over her hair because the more she looked at it, the more it began to seem too vulgar-bright.

The night was blustery with wind. The lilac tree at the gate dipped and swayed, sending leaves scurrying off down the lane. A tiny moon sailed in and out of the clouds above.

Agatha looked ruefully at John's dark cottage. She felt that she would have liked him to go along with her. The road to Ancombe was quiet. She passed only two cars on the way and one late-night rambler, trudging along, scarf over the lower part of the face as protection against the wind.

When Agatha parked outside Peggy's cottage and saw that all the lights were on and music was blaring out, she experienced a feeling of relief. Peggy was obviously entertaining. Still, thought Agatha, having come this far, I may as well see if she'll give me a hint of what she has found out. If I handle it properly, she may be tempted to brag.

She walked up the garden path where plaster gnomes

leered at her from the shrubbery. The Village People were belting out "Y.M.C.A." The door was standing slightly ajar. Agatha walked into the little hall. The music crashed about her ears but she could not hear any voices.

Suddenly frightened, she pushed open the door of the living-room and reeled before the increased blast of noise. She walked over to the stereo and switched it off. Now the silence, broken only by the sound of the peeing statue and the wind outside, was more frightening than the noise of the music.

"Peggy!" croaked Agatha. She cleared her throat and shouted loudly, "Peggy!"

Agatha looked longingly at the phone, which was in the shape of a shoe. Call the police before you look any further, she told herself. But something impelled her to go out and across the hall and push open the kitchen door at the back . . . She fumbled inside the door for a light switch and, finding it, pressed it down. Fluorescent light blazed down on the kitchen . . . on the blood on the white walls, on the blood on the floor and on the savagely cut body of Peggy Slither lying by the back door.

Agatha let out a whimper and stood with her hand to her mouth. She forced herself to kneel down by that terrible body and feel for a pulse. No life. No life at all.

She rose and scrambled back to the living-room and seized the phone and dialled the police. Then she went outside and leaned her head against the cold wall of the cottage.

# EIGHT

†

FOR the next two weeks, Carsely was a village under siege. It was flooded by press and by sightseers. Finally rough weather drove the sightseers away, leaving behind them soda cans and sandwich wrappers, and another Balkan uprising sent the press rushing back to London. It was a relief to walk down the village streets without being accosted by reporters. The members of the ladies' society picked up all the rubbish left behind and bagged it. Even John Fletcher, landlord of the Red Lion, who had done a roaring trade, was glad to see the last of the press and the gawking public.

John Armitage had returned from London as soon as he had heard the news of the latest murder. Agatha was once more restored to a brunette, having gone straight to the hairdresser's the day after the murder and right after signing her statement at police headquarters in Mircester. Only the dogged police were left, still going from house to house in Carsely and in the neighbouring villages, questioning everyone over and over again. The weapon with which Peggy had been so brutally murdered had never been found.

Agatha had expected John to be a frequent caller to discuss the case, but he seemed quiet and withdrawn, saying he was behind with his writing and had to catch up. She herself had been frightened into inactivity, although she would not admit it to herself. Such as Agatha Raisin hardly ever admitted to being frightened. She persuaded herself that three murders were just too much. Out there was a madman who should be left to the police. But she lost weight through nerves, waking up during the night at the slightest sound and picking at her food during the day.

Mrs. Bloxby had given up urging Agatha to find the killer. "It really is not safe for you, Mrs. Raisin," she said. "What if this dreadful murderer should decide you knew something as well?"

The day after the press had gone, John Armitage called round. "Are you eating?" he asked anxiously, as if noticing Agatha properly for the first time since his return from London. "You look haggard."

Agatha glared at him. Despite her fright, she had been pleased with her new slimline figure. "I did find the body," she snapped.

John sat down at her kitchen table. "And what about you?" asked Agatha. "What have you been doing?"

"I told you. Writing and more writing."

"But you've never said anything about how you got on in London."

"There's nothing much to tell. I saw my publisher, I saw my agent, I saw my friends . . ."

"And you had at least one dinner with Charlotte Bellinge."

"How did you know that?"

"There was a parcel sticking out of your letter-box. I opened your door to put it on the table and heard her dulcet tones on your answering machine."

He coloured faintly. "I thought there might be a lead there, but there was nothing further to add. I did go back to see that vicar at New Cross, but he said he was busy and slammed the door in my face."

"Don't you find that suspicious?"

"Not really. I think he's guilty about having lied to us in the first place. Anyway, to get back to Peggy Slither. She thought she had found out something. And you saw nothing around her home before you found the body? No sinister men?"

"Nothing."

"Any cars on the road?"

Agatha frowned in thought. "Two passed me going away from Ancombe but don't ask me the colour or make. It was dark and I didn't notice them in particular."

Suddenly, in her mind's eye, she was driving towards Ancombe that evening. "The rambler," she exclaimed. "I forgot about the rambler."

"What rambler? Did you tell the police?"

"No, I forgot about him. The shock of finding Peggy lying in all that blood drove him right out of my head."

"What was he like?" asked John eagerly.

"I just got a glimpse. One of those dark woolly hats and a scarf over the lower part of his face. An anorak, a backpack, dark trousers."

"A scarf over his face and you didn't think that suspicious?"

"There was a freezing wind that night. Oh, God, I'd better tell the police. They'll think me such a fool for forgetting."

The doorbell rang. "You get it, John," said Agatha. "Probably some lingering local reporter. To think of the days when I cultivated the press!"

John went to the door and came back a few moments later followed by Bill Wong.

"There you are Agatha, you want the police and here's Bill."

"Why do you want the police?" asked Bill, shrugging off his raincoat and placing it on a chair.

"I've just remembered something." Agatha told him about the rambler.

"Agatha!" Bill sounded exasperated. "Why didn't you remember this before? I'm off duty, but get me a piece of paper. I'll need to take this down."

Agatha went through to her desk and came back with a sheet of paper and then sat down and described the rambler.

"Do you know what I think?" Bill put down his pen with a sigh. "I think our murderer was very lucky. Wilkes is going to be furious when I tell him this. If you had told us right away on the night of the murder, we could have put up road-blocks, we could have scoured the countryside for him. I'd best get off. We'll put out a police bulletin asking him to come forward." He got to his feet and put on his coat.

"Where was Alf Bloxby on the evening of the murder?" asked John.

"According to his wife, he was out on his rounds all evening. We've interviewed all the people he said he'd been to see, but it still leaves an hour unaccounted for."

"Mrs. Bloxby never told me that." Agatha experienced a pang of unease. "What does the vicar say he was doing during that hour?"

"He says he was just walking about. He says the whole business of Tristan's murder had upset him dreadfully and he felt like taking a good walk before bedtime to clear his head."

"Sounds reasonable," said Agatha. She followed him to the door. "Why did you call?"

"Social visit."

"How's Alice?"

"She's fine."

"Take her to see your parents?"

"Yes. They loved her."

Oh dear, thought Agatha.

She saw him out and returned to the kitchen. "Why did you ask about Alf Bloxby?" she demanded.

"I've been thinking. Just because we love Mrs. Bloxby doesn't mean we know anything about Alf. Do you?"

"No, I don't know much, but I do know this. Such as Mrs. Bloxby would never, ever stay married to any man capable of murder."

"She might not know he was capable of murder."

"Rubbish."

"I mean, did she say anything to you about Alf being unable to account for an hour of his movements?"

"He did account for them!"

"But only his word. No witnesses. Let's go and see her."

"All right. If it'll make you feel any better."

"You're not wearing your ring."

"Oh, that. I'd forgotten about it. Do you want me to put it on?"

"May as well maintain the fiction."

"We don't need to maintain it in front of Mrs. Bloxby."

"But we do in front of other people," said John.

Agatha went through to her desk and fished out the ring and put it on her finger. It felt loose. Good heavens, she thought, I'm even losing weight on my fingers.

Leaves wheeled and whirled about them as they walked to

the vicarage. To Agatha, the village no longer felt like a safe haven. She felt there was menace lurking around every corner. She longed for a cigarette and remembered the days when one never, ever smoked in the street. Now the street was about the only place outside one's own home where one could smoke.

Mrs. Bloxby opened the door to them. "Come in quietly," she said. "Alf is resting."

They followed her into the vicarage sitting-room. Agatha and Mrs. Bloxby surveyed each other. Mrs. Bloxby noticed that Agatha was considerably thinner and Agatha noticed that Mrs. Bloxby's usually mild eyes held a haunted look. They had talked since the murder, but only briefly.

Agatha told her about the rambler and Mrs. Bloxby clasped her hands as if in prayer. "If only you had remembered this earlier, Mrs. Raisin."

"They're putting out a bulletin, asking him to come forward," said John. "If he's innocent, he will."

"I've been thinking about ramblers," said Agatha. "I mean, one never really notices them."

"Not groups of ramblers," commented Mrs. Bloxby with a certain edge in her voice. "But one, on his own, at night!"

"I know, I know," mourned Agatha. "But the horror of Peggy's murder drove it right out of my mind until today."

"Bill was round this morning," said John. "He says there is a whole hour your husband can't account for."

"Most of us have whole hours in our lives we can't account for," said Mrs. Bloxby. "It's just unlucky for Alf his hour should have happened on the evening Peggy was murdered. All this is wearing my husband down. I could do without your suspicions being added to our worries, Mr. Armitage."

"I didn't—"

"Yes, you did," interrupted Mrs. Bloxby. She rounded on Agatha. "I thought you had given up investigating."

"I had," said Agatha, silently cursing John.

"Whoever is committing these murders is highly dangerous. I suggest you both leave it to the police. Now, if you don't mind, I have things to do."

They both left the vicarage, Agatha furious with John. "I never should have gone along with you," she said. "Mrs. Bloxby is my best friend."

"Never mind. It's lunch-time and you look a ghost of your former self. We'll go to the pub and have something."

Agatha was about to say pettishly that she didn't want to go with him, but realized she was reluctant to be on her own. "All right," she said ungraciously. "But I don't want much."

In the pub, they both ordered shepherd's pie. Although there were quite a few regulars at the bar, there wasn't much conversation. The murders had poisoned the atmosphere.

Agatha surprised herself by eating all the food on her plate. She decided it was time she went in for some decent home cooking instead of microwave meals.

When they had finished, she looked curiously at John. "You are strangely reticent about Charlotte Bellinge."

"If I had anything relating to the case to tell you, Agatha, I would."

"I don't think you went to see her because you thought she had anything to add. I think you're smitten with her."

"She is a very attractive woman, but no, I am not smitten with her."

"So she rejected your advances?"

"Don't be cheeky, Agatha. We're only pretending to be engaged. You have no right to question me on my personal life."

This was indeed true but for some reason Agatha did not want to be reminded of it.

"So you told me briefly before that you'd been to see Mrs. Essex and Mrs. Tremp. Nothing there, I gathered."

"No, except the wine."

"What wine?"

Agatha told him about the home-made wine and the odd effect it had had on her.

"That's interesting," said John. "You mean, Miss Jellop may have given Tristan some and he might have told her things he wouldn't otherwise have said?"

"Could be."

John sighed. "And now she's dead, we'll never know. What about Mrs. Tremp? There was something cold-blooded about the way she talked about her husband's death. If a woman can sit looking at her husband who's just had a stroke without immediately calling an ambulance, then she must be really pretty tough."

"I don't know. I kept the discussion to the duck races. She seemed pretty friendly and normal."

"Did she know Peggy Slither?"

"I don't know."

"Let's go and ask her."

"I somehow don't want anyone to know we're still investigating," said Agatha.

"You told me she was going to bake cakes for the big event. We'll ask her how she's getting on."

"I suppose we could do that."


After they had returned to Lilac Lane and had driven off in John's car, Agatha felt the black edges of depression hovering around her. For years she had been driven by her obsession for James Lacey, getting James Lacey, and marrying James Lacey. Then she had been divorced by him. After that, she lived in dreams that one day he would return to her. Cold reality was telling her he would never return. Carsely had become a sinister place. She was going to interview a woman who probably did not know anything at all relevant to the case with a man she was pretending to be engaged to. Bill Wong, who had been a sort of soul mate in that he was always being rejected by the loves of his life, had at last found one who evidently could stand up to his parents.

"What's up?" asked John.

"Nothing. Why?"

"This car's filling up with gloom and it's coming from you."

"I've got a bit of a headache, that's all."

"Want to go back home and take some aspirin?"

"No, I'll be all right. Here we are. She's probably at home. I don't think she goes out much."

They parked and got out of the car. The door was standing open. Agatha rang the bell beside the door. The bell shrilled somewhere inside the house.

"That's odd," said John. "She must be in. Try again."

Agatha rang the bell and waited.

"I think we'd better take a look inside," said John uneasily.

Agatha walked in first. "Mrs. Tremp!" she called. No reply. Outside, the rooks cawed from their tree and the wind rushed around the converted barn.

Followed by John, she walked into the kitchen and let out a scream. Mrs. Tremp was lying stretched out on the floor, her eyes closed and her hands folded on her breast.

"See if she's alive," said John, tugging a mobile phone out of his pocket. "I'll call the police."

Mrs. Tremp opened her eyes at that moment and struggled to her feet. "It is my meditation hour," she said crossly. "I do not like to be disturbed. I hoped you would go away." She smoothed down her tweed skirt with her hands. "What do you want?"

Agatha sank down onto a kitchen chair. "I just wanted to

ask if you could cope with all the cake baking for the duck race."

"Of course," said Mrs. Tremp. "I would have told you if I could not. How are the arrangements going?"

"I'm on my way to see Farmer Brent," said Agatha.

"You mean you haven't got permission from him yet? You'd better hurry up. It's only three weeks to the races."

"Isn't it terrible about Peggy Slither?" said John.

"Oh, her." Mrs. Tremp gave a disdainful sniff. "Probably her ex-husband. He was furious at having to pay out so much after the divorce proceedings."

"Did you know her?" asked Agatha.

"Tristan took me over to meet her once. Disgusting, vulgar woman."

"I gather Tristan was friendly with her."

"She was so rude to me that Tristan assured me he would have nothing more to do with her."

"And you haven't heard from her since?"

"Why should I? Such as Mrs. Slither and such as myself have absolutely nothing in common. Now I do have things to do. I suggest you get Mr. Brent's permission as soon as possible."

"We couldn't really stay to get more out of her," said John as they drove on to Brent's farm at the top of the hill.

"She's got a study off the hall," said Agatha. "The door was open and I looked in as we went out. There's a desk there with letters and correspondence. I'd love to have a look at them. I think she's hiding something. I wonder if Tristan ever wrote to her."

"Why should he?" asked John. "I mean, he was in the same village."

"Still, I wouldn't mind having a look. Maybe she wrote to someone about him."

"Then the someone will have the letter. Not Mrs. Tremp."

"There was a computer on the desk. Maybe she's got letters logged in it. The days when it was considered bad manners to type a letter to a friend have long gone."

"I don't know how you're ever going to have a chance to look at them."

"Maybe. I wonder if she locks her door at night."

"Meaning," said John, "you plan to creep in one night and have a look? Don't be silly. There'd be all hell to pay if you were caught. Is that the entrance to Brent's farm on the left?"

"Yes, let's hope he's at home. I don't feel like trekking over muddy fields looking for him."

To her relief, Mark Brent opened the door to them himself.

"I was just about to have a cup of tea," he said. He was a tall, thin man with long arms and stooped shoulders. His thick hair was grey and his long face burnt red by working outdoors. "The wife's off visiting her sister," he said. He prepared a pot of tea and put mugs and milk and sugar on the table. "Sit down," he said. "Isn't it awful about these murders? Is that why you're here, Mrs. Raisin?"

"No," said Agatha. "It's about these duck races. I remember you had an event for the boy scouts in one of your fields with a pretty stream running through it." She told him all about the duck races.

"It's all yours," said Brent. "There's cattle in that field but I'll move them for the day. When is it to be held?"

"October twenty-third."

"Fine. I like to do my bit. Help yourselves. I'm glad I'm outside the village. It's as if that there damned curate and his poncy ways brought something evil in with him."

"You knew Tristan?" asked Agatha.

"My wife, Gladys, was friendly with him. I'd come in from the fields and there they'd be, laughing and joking, and Gladys looking like a dog's dinner, all tarted up in her Sunday best although it was a weekday. Then she tells me she wants a cheque for this Tristan. She says he could invest money for us and make a killing. I said the only killing was going to be Tristan himself. There was something slimy about him. So I got him one day in the village and told him if he came near my wife again I'd set the dogs on him. Poor Gladys cried and cried when I told her and called me a monster.

" 'I put up with it,' I says, 'until he tried to get money out of you.' Fact is, she thought he fancied her. Now don't get me wrong. My Gladys is a fine-looking woman but she's in her fifties." He looked at Agatha. "Didn't have you fooled as well, did he, Mrs. Raisin? I heard how you had dinner with him the night he was murdered."

"No," said Agatha. "He did suggest investing money for me but I refused."

"And I hear you pair are engaged?"

"That's right," said Agatha. "How did you hear that?"

"All over the village, it is. Good on you. I wish you both well. You'll be getting married in the church. Nothing like a good old-fashioned village wedding."

"You didn't threaten to kill Tristan?" asked John.

"Meaning, did I stick a knife in him? No, that's not my way. A telling-off was enough."

"I didn't mean . . ."

"I know what you meant," said the farmer with unimpaired good humour. "Our Mrs. Raisin here has made a name for herself as a detective. Seems as if you're well-suited."

"I found Peggy Slither," said Agatha. "On the road to Ancombe, I noticed this rambler. I've only just remembered and told the police. You didn't at any time see anyone strange about the village?"

"Not on the days of the murders. We're not a tourist place like Broadway. We get these chaps selling kitchen stuff round the doors. Then there are women from the Red Cross and the Lifeboat people come round collecting. Ramblers, of course. Few outsiders at the bed-and-breakfast places, but I gather the police have checked them all out. I think all of us have had the police round asking questions three or four times. But I tell you this, Mrs. Raisin." His voice became hard. "Whoever is doing these here murders is a dangerous man. I think you should sit this one out and leave it to the police. Don't want you getting hurt."

"Sounds like a threat," said John.

"Just a bit of sensible advice. Now I'd best get out there. There's fencing to be repaired."

"I think that *was* a threat," said Agatha as they drove off.

"I don't know. Seems a straightforward-enough man to me."

Agatha sighed. "Well, I'd better throw myself into the publicity for these duck races. I'll be round at Mrs. Bloxby's if you want me."

"Right. I'll get on with some more writing."

Agatha spent the afternoon discussing arrangements such as the hiring of a marquee with Mrs. Bloxby and phoning up local papers, arranging advertisements for the duck races to go in and also for free publicity. But once a public relations officer, always a public relations officer. She also sent press handouts to all the nationals and TV stations to the effect that the murder village was returning to normal. Might get a few of them down from London.

It was only that evening that her thoughts turned to Mrs. Tremp's desk. No one in the village would leave their doors open at night after three murders. But country people often left a spare key in the gutter or under the doormat or in a flowerpot. Had Agatha not felt the black edges of depression returning, she would never have decided to try to break into Mrs. Tremp's home. But action and thoughts of action kept the depression at bay. She set her alarm for two in the morning but she was so restless that she only fell asleep at twelve-thirty and woke at the alarm's shrill sound feeling groggy.

She dressed in dark clothes and decided to walk. Thank goodness Mrs. Tremp doesn't keep a dog, she thought, as she finally reached the converted barn. The guttering was too high up for anyone to reach and there was no doormat or flowerpot. Frustrated and not wanting to turn back now she had come so far, she walked round the side of the house. That must be the study window, she thought. Easy to break a pane of glass and release the catch, but that would mean Mrs. Tremp might hear the noise. Shining the light of a pencil torch at the ground to make sure she did not trip over anything, she made her way round to the back of the house. At the back there was a trapdoor in the ground with coal dust around it. She eased back the bolt and lifted the trapdoor and looked down. Coal had been delivered recently and glittered with reptilian blackness in the faint beam of her torch. She eased herself down onto the top of the pile. The coal began to slide under her feet. She reached upwards trying to catch the top of the trapdoor but she was descending too fast, crashing down among rumbling lumps of coal to finally land at the bottom of the cellar. She lay there, her heart thumping. She had lost her torch but there was faint light from the open trapdoor. She crawled to her feet, feeling bruised. She could dimly make out a stone staircase.

Agatha was just creeping towards it when she heard from

above someone running down the stairs and then a key being turned in the cellar door. Then she heard the front door of the house opening and footsteps hurrying round the side of the house. Agatha scrambled away from the coal and into a corner piled with old suitcases and boxes. Mrs. Tremp's voice said triumphantly, "Got you. You can wait in there until the police come." She slammed down the trapdoor and Agatha could hear her shooting the bolt across.

Agatha felt her way across the floor on her hands and knees with the mad idea of trying to climb up the coal stack and force the trapdoor. Her hand touched her lost torch and she grabbed it eagerly. No, she could not force the trapdoor. She must hide somewhere, somewhere the police would not find her. The beam of the torch lit on a rusty suit of armour covered in coal dust. In a mad panic, Agatha hauled the suit upright. It was unusually light. Probably a replica. She lifted off the helmet and headpiece. Standing on one of the old suitcases, and putting the legs of the suit at an angle, she eased herself into them. She put on the breastplate and fastened it with the leather straps at the back. Then she put on the gauntlets and lifted the headpiece over her head and with a trembling hand forced the rusty visor down, shuffled off into the corner and stood there.

It was then she realized that because of the murders it wouldn't be one local policeman from Moreton-in-Marsh who would arrive but probably the whole squad from Mircester.

She stood there, trembling with cold and fright until she heard the wail of police sirens drawing closer and closer. Then Mrs. Tremp's voice shrill with excitement. "I've got him locked in the cellar. He can't get out."

The cellar door opened, the light was switched on. There was a light switch at the top of the stairs, thought Agatha. But Mrs. Tremp had sounded the alarm before I could have reached it. Bill Wong was there with Wilkes. Four policemen were systematically going through the cellar, turning over boxes, raking over the coal. Coal dust rose in the air. Agatha prayed she would not sneeze.

And then Bill Wong walked over to the suit of armour which encased the trembling Agatha. He raised the visor. A pair of terrified bearlike eyes stared back at him. Bill slammed down the visor.

"Nothing here," he said.

After the search was over, Agatha could hear Wilkes complaining that everyone around was getting hysterical and that Mrs. Tremp had probably left the trapdoor open herself or the coalman had. She had said a load of coal had been delivered only that day. The coal must have shifted and tumbled down in the night. At last Agatha was left alone. She lifted off the visor, took off the gauntlets and headpiece, and lay against a pile of boxes and eased out of the armoured legs. The house was silent again. She crept up the cellar stairs and tried the door. It was unlocked. Agatha walked through a laundry room and then into the hall. All she wanted to do now was escape. She tiptoed to the front door and gently unlocked it and slid back the bolt. Mrs. Tremp would just have to think that in all the excitement she had forgotten to lock the door.

She hurried down the hill, keeping to the shadow of the trees. She let out a sob of relief when she turned into Lilac Lane. She reached her cottage door and put her key in the lock. A voice in her ear said, "What the hell were you playing at?"

Agatha gave a stifled scream and turned round. Bill Wong's eyes gleamed at her in the darkness.

"Oh, Bill," babbled Agatha. "I'm so sorry. So very sorry."

"Let's go inside. You've some explaining to do."

In the fluorescent light of the kitchen, Agatha was a sorry

sight. She was black with coal dust. "I'd let you clean yourself up first," said Bill. "But I'm in a hurry."

Agatha seized a handful of kitchen paper and ran it under the cold tap and then wiped her face and hands.

She sat down at the kitchen table. "Bill, thank you for not betraying me."

"I should have done," he said grimly. "This could cost me my job if anything came out. Lucky for you that Mrs. Tremp came to the conclusion that the coalman had left that trapdoor open and rats or something had shifted the coal during the night. She was most apologetic. So, what have you been up to?"

In a halting voice, Agatha told him all about her plan to look at the papers on Mrs. Tremp's desk and also to see what was in her computer.

"Now, listen to me very carefully," said Bill. "If I ever catch you doing anything like that again, I will not only have you arrested, our friendship will be at an end. I risked my job for you, Agatha. Of all the stupid things to do! This is one case you are going to leave strictly alone from now on. If you do hear of anything relevant to the case, then you are to tell me immediately. I am going to get some sleep with what is left of the night."

"Any news of the rambler?"

"Lucky for you, there is. He walked into police headquarters around seven o'clock this evening—I mean, yesterday evening. Respectable computer nerd, member of a rambling society, said he liked night walking on his own occasionally. No record."

"Why lucky for me?"

"If no one had turned up, it would have looked as if that faulty memory of yours had lost us the chance of getting the killer. Before I go. Why Mrs. Tremp? Did she say something you aren't telling me about?"

"John and I saw her earlier in the day. Tristan had taken her once to meet Peggy Slither. There's something not quite right about Mrs. Tremp. When her husband had his fatal stroke, she sat watching him for a bit before calling the ambulance. She seemed to be . . . well . . . gleeful that he was dead."

"And that's all you had to go on?"

"I know it sounds silly, but I've had good hunches before."

"Agatha, for the last time, leave it alone."

"Okay," said Agatha wearily. She saw him to the door. "Give my regards to Alice."

His tired face lit up. "Thanks. I will."

Agatha shut and locked the door behind him and set the burglar alarm. Then she crawled wearily up the stairs and stripped off her dirty clothes and threw them in the laundry basket before taking a shower and scrubbing off all the coal dust.

Her last thought before she fell asleep was that she was actually relieved she could leave this messy and dreadful case alone.


Next day Agatha went to a printer's where she got a flyer she had run off on her computer enlarged. She collected two hundred copies and spent an afternoon posting them up in shop windows and on trees in Carsely and in the villages round about.

When she returned home, John rang and said he'd be round in a few minutes.

"I've been thinking," he said as he walked in, "that perhaps we've been neglecting the London end. We never found out who beat Tristan up in New Cross."

"Forget it," said Agatha. "I have been told in no uncertain terms to keep away from everything and anything to do with the case. And by the way, that rambler I saw was kosher. A respectable citizen."

"Why are you warned off? What's been happening?"

"I may as well tell you." Agatha described the events of the night. John was hardly able to hear the rest of her story, he was laughing so hard. "You are an idiot," he said finally. "Thank goodness you didn't drag me into it. Not that I would have gone with you. But I haven't been warned off."

"I should think the warning applies to you as well."

"So you're just giving up? Have you ever given up before?"

"No, but I've never been at such a dead end before. I tell you, John, I'm going to concentrate on these duck races and make it all a success for Mrs. Bloxby and then find something safe and pleasant to do with my time."

"Like what?"

"I'll think of something."

"I think I'll go back up to London," said John, "and see what I can find out. Want to come with me?"

Agatha shook her head. "I've given up."

# NINE

†

THE day of the duck races was fine. Hazy sunshine gilded the countryside. Agatha was there early to supervise the arrangements. John had said he would join her later.

Miss Simms was to sell programmes at the field gate. Six races were to be run. The entrance fee was one pound, but as Agatha had put a sign up on the main road saying FREE DRINKS, she was sure that the entrance charge would not deter the crowd. The free drinks were to be fruit punch laced with Miss Jellop's wine. The bottles of wine could be bought for three pounds each. The ducks, for anyone wanting to take part in the race, were to be sold for two pounds each. One of Miss Simms's ex-lovers, a bookie, had volunteered to take the racing bets. Agatha had donated small engraved silver cups to be given to the winner of each race. Agatha was glad the day was warm because the three men who had volunteered to start the duck races would have to stand in the stream in their bare feet to lift the restraining plank across the stream which held the ducks at the starting line.

Agatha was glad she had trusted the weather report and had cancelled the marquee. The day set fair without a breath of wind. The sun sparkled on the rushing stream and shone on the red and yellow leaves of the trees bordering the field.

Some of the local farmers, along with Farmer Brent, had set up tables to sell meat and local vegetables. Mrs. Tremp had two tables, one with home-made jam and the other with cakes.

Agatha mixed fruit juice and two bottles of Miss Jellop's wine into a giant punch-bowl, ready to be ladled into small plastic cups. The event was to start at ten. A small trickle of people began to enter the field. Agatha noticed old Mrs. Feathers. Why didn't I think to question her about Tristan? she wondered. But deep down she knew it was because Mrs. Feathers was old and frail and Agatha was ashamed when she remembered the trouble the old woman had gone to producing that expensive dinner. More people arrived and Agatha was suddenly very busy ladling out punch and selling wine. John appeared and she appealed to him for help because a large crowd of people were demanding punch.

Although Agatha had vowed to have nothing more to do with the case, she could not help turning over what she knew in her mind. There were noisy cheers from the stream where the races were taking place. The bookie was doing well, taking bets. After the first hour, Mrs. Tremp had sold practically everything. More and more people were arriving, drawn by the offer of free drink. Agatha began to feel marginalized. After all, she had paid for the cups. She should be the one to present them. But it was Mrs. Bloxby who was making the presentations.

Agatha tried to console herself with the thought that the day had turned out to be a roaring success. But the press were there in force and she was getting none of the glory.

John tugged out his mobile phone. "Won't be moment," he said. "Just phoning home to see if there are any messages."

"All right. But hurry up," said Agatha sulkily. Then she thought about mobile phones. What had people ever done without them? A thin woman a little away from her was shouting into one. Doesn't need a phone, thought Agatha. Her voice is loud enough to carry miles.

And then she stood with her mouth a little open, the ladle in her hand while a customer looked at her impatiently.

Had Tristan had a mobile phone? If he had, could someone have phoned him the night he died and threatened him? But the police would have found it and checked the numbers.

"Are you going to give me any of that punch or not?" demanded a man in front of her.

"Sure." Agatha ladled some into a cup. She realized she had served the same man about five times before. The crowd was getting noisy and boisterous. Agatha, seeing the punch-bowl was nearly empty, added a bottle of wine and fruit juice to fill it up again. Perhaps two bottles of the stuff had been too strong. A team of Morris dancers had just arrived in their flow-ered hats and jingling bells and started buying bottles of wine. "I don't have a spare corkscrew," said Agatha uneasily. She had not imagined that anyone would drink that lethal stuff until they got home. "Got one here," said a red-faced Morris dancer and his friends all cheered.

Over the Tannoy came an announcement that there would be a break for lunch. Agatha picked a placard off the ground at her feet which said CLOSED FOR LUNCH and placed it on the table. "Do you think anyone will pinch anything?" asked John.

"We'll put the bottles back in the boxes for now and tape them over."

The members of the ladies' societies had set up a buffet at the far corner of the field and had laid out tables and chairs.

Mrs. Bloxby came up to Agatha, her eyes shining. "Such a success," she said. "We were going to confine it to six races, but we've decided to hold more in the afternoon and finish with the Morris dancers.

"What about prizes?" asked Agatha. "Surely all the cups have gone."

"I thought we might present each winner with two bottles of wine."

"Good idea," said Agatha in a flat voice because she still thought that she should have been the one to present the prizes.

"And seeing as the organization has been largely done by you, Mrs. Raisin, I thought it would be nice if you could address the crowd at the end."

Agatha brightened visibly.

When Mrs. Bloxby had left, John said, "What now? Do we go over there and fight for something to eat?"

"I wonder if you could get me a plate of something, John. I want to speak to Mrs. Feathers."

"What about?" he demanded sharply. "I thought you had given up."

"Just one question. I'll tell you later."

Agatha began to search. Mrs. Feathers was not with the lunch crowd nor among the people still crowding in front of the farmers' stalls, Agatha being the only one who had packed up for lunch. And then she saw her grey head bobbing along in the direction of the gate. She ran after her, shouting, "Mrs. Feathers!"

The old lady turned around slowly, blinking in the sunlight. "Oh, it's you, Mrs. Raisin. Lovely day."

"Yes, it is. We're very lucky. Mrs. Feathers, did Tristan have a mobile phone?"

"I was sure he had. But I must have been mistaken. He always used mine."

"What makes you think he had one?"

"I went into his flat one day when I thought he was out, to change the bed linen. But he was in and he was using a mobile phone. He put it away quickly when he saw me. Later when he came down to use the phone, I asked him why he didn't use his own phone and he said it had been a friend's and he had returned it. It was a terrible business, that murder. It really shook me up."

"And Tristan never at any time said anything that you might think would give the police a clue to his murder?"

"Oh, no, they've asked me and asked me. Dear Tristan. He said I was like a mother to him."

"I'm sure you were," said Agatha. "When's the funeral?"

"That took place some time ago. A cousin arranged it."

Drat, thought Agatha, I'd forgotten all about the funeral. But what good would that have done me?

"Do you have a name and address for this cousin?"

"Reckon as how you'll need to ask the police, m'dear. They took away all his stuff and then I think they sent it on to the cousin."

Agatha thanked her and was about to turn away when she saw Bill and Alice just paying their entrance fees.

"Bill," said Agatha, approaching him. "Could I have a word?"

"What about?" demanded Alice.

Agatha looked at Bill pleadingly. "It's a police matter."

"All right. Alice, go and see if there's anything at the stall that Mother would like."

Alice shot Agatha a venomous look and trudged off.

Agatha told Bill about the mobile phone. "Good work," he said. "I'll get them on to it. They can check all the mobile phone companies and see which one he was registered with. But I thought I told you to stop investigating."

"It just came up in conversation with Mrs. Feathers," said Agatha. "Oh, here's your beloved back again."

"I want a drink," said Alice, "but that stall is closed."

God forgive me for what I am about to do, thought Agatha. "I'll get you a drink, Alice." She went to her stall and drew the cork on a bottle of home-made wine while Bill had pulled out his mobile and was phoning headquarters. She picked up one of the large tumblers she had kept for people who only wanted fruit juice and filled it up. "I'd tell Bill that's just punch," said Agatha. "It's pretty strong stuff."

"I can drink any man under the table," sneered Alice. She went back to join Bill.

John came back with a plate of ham and salad, which he handed to Agatha. "Thanks," she said.

"What's going on?" asked John. "When I was queuing up, I saw you talking to Bill and he looked very serious."

Agatha told him about the mobile phone. "That might be something," said John. "Say he had his phone beside the bed. Someone phones him after you left and frightens him. He decides to make a run for it, but first of all, he thinks he'll take that money out of the church box. Whoever threatened him is watching the house, follows him to the vicar's study and stabs him."

"Could be. Oh, they're starting up again and I haven't had time to eat."

"You go ahead. I'll cope with the first lot and then you take over so that I can eat something."

Agatha walked over towards the duck races carrying her plate. People were cheering on the ducks, bets were being laid. The little yellow plastic ducks were bobbing down the stream, occasionally swirling round in the eddies. Agatha found it too difficult to eat with just one plastic fork, so she headed for the lunch tables and found a chair. A little way away from her the Morris men were downing glasses of Miss Jellop's wine, their faces flushed and their voices loud.

"Mrs. Raisin? It is Agatha Raisin, isn't it?"

Agatha looked up. A pretty young woman was standing over her holding a child by the hand. With a wrench of memory, Agatha said, "Bunty! How are you?"

The woman seated next to Agatha moved away and Bunty sat down and put the child on her knee.

Bunty had been Agatha's last secretary before she retired. "Is that yours?" asked Agatha, pointing with her fork to the little girl Bunty was holding.

"Yes, this is Philippa."

"Who did you marry?"

"Philip Jervsey."

"Of Jervsey Advertising?"

"That's the one. After you packed up and retired, I took a job as his secretary."

Agatha frowned. "I thought he was married."

"Yes, he was . . . then."

"Did he get a divorce to marry you?" asked Agatha, ever curious.

"Yes. I feel guilty about it. But I was mad about him. Still am. I took my time about saying yes. You know how it is, Agatha, secretaries and bosses. It gets like a marriage. You get to know them better than their wives."

"Was it a bitter divorce?"

"Not too bad. Cost him a lot, though. But there were no children. We've got a place over in Cirencester we use for weekends. Give Philippa here some country air. And what about you? I see your name from time to time in the newspapers. Death does seem to follow you around." She looked at the ring sparkling on Agatha's finger. "Are you married?"

"I was. I'm divorced. I still wear my rings." Agatha did not want to talk about John.

Bunty looked around. "It all looks so peaceful here. You wouldn't think there had been any murders in such a quiet rural spot. Have the police any idea who did it?"

Agatha shook her head. Philippa squirmed on her mother's knee. "I want to see the ducks," she wailed.

"I'd better take her or I'll get no peace." Bunty rose to her feet. "Nice to see you again."

Agatha saw Alice sitting a little way away on her own, drinking wine. She must have bought a whole bottle from John. There was no sign of Bill. He was probably off somewhere phoning to see if there was any news about that mobile phone. She finished her food and went back to where John was ladling out punch. "We'd better stop selling that wine," he said when he saw her. "The Morris men won't be able to dance if they have any more."

"Are we selling much?"

"Yes, quite a lot. But people are mostly taking it home."

"We'll put the bottles on the table in the boxes and if the Morris men come back, tell them we're sold out and we'll keep on selling it when they go away."

The afternoon wore on and a chill crept into the air. Mrs. Bloxby came up. "The Morris men are getting ready to perform and then it's your speech, Agatha. You may as well close up here. You've done splendidly."

Agatha thankfully put a CLOSED sign on the table and she and John put the remaining plastic cups in a box.

They walked to where the crowd was gathering to watch the Morris men. Bill and Alice were standing just behind the crowd and Alice was red-faced and shouting at him. "You're nothing but a mother's boy."

"Let's go round the other side. I don't want to listen to this," said Agatha. She felt guilty. She should have warned Alice about the effects of the wine.

They found a space where they could watch the Morris men. Alf Bloxby's voice sounded over the crowd. "We will now see a performance of the stick dance by the Mircester Morris Men. Morris dancing is one of the characteristic folk dances of England. We do not know its origins, although we know it was derived from agrarian traditions of fertility rites and celebrations at sowing and at harvest time."

A Morris man fell over and lay on the grass.

"Though well-known during Shakespeare's time," continued the vicar, "it almost died away during the Industrial Revolution, but has now thankfully been revived. You will enjoy the colourful sight of the dancers with their bells and waving hankies dancing to tunes played on the fiddle, pipe and tabor and melodeon. Over to you, boys."

The Morris man who had fallen over was dragged to his feet and he stood there, blinking in the fading sunlight. A tape was put into a player and the jingly, jaunty tune of Morris music sounded out. The dancers with flowers in their hats and silver bells at their knees clutched their sticks and faced each other. They were supposed to bang their crossed sticks as they met in the dance but two of them missed and hit their opposite number a thwack. "You did that o' purpose, Fred," yelled one, and seizing his stick brought it down on the unfortunate Fred's head. Soon the dance had degenerated into a rumble.

Alf Bloxby tried to separate the warring dancers but was thrust aside with cries of "Get away, you murderer."

The vicar, his face flaming, looked around for help, shouting to the crowd to stop laughing and do something.

"Police!" shouted Bill Wong. Alf switched off the music. The dancers stopped hitting each other and stood there sheepishly.

Bill shouted to the crowd. "All of you, go home. Show's over."

The crowd began to stream off towards the gate. "My speech," wailed Agatha.

"Too late," said John. "We'd better get back and start loading up the rest of the wine and stuff." John had borrowed a trailer which was hitched to his car, parked at the edge of the field.

John stared at the ground behind the table. "Agatha, the wine's gone. Someone's nicked the rest of it."

"I don't care," said Agatha. "I hope it poisons them."

"But we'd better tell Bill!"

"Bill's got his hands full. You didn't leave the money behind?"

"No, I've got it here in a bag. We'll count it out at home and then take it along to the vicarage. Are you sure you don't want to report the missing wine?"

"I'm sure. Just let's hope it wasn't a married couple who took it. A few slugs of that wine and they'll be in the divorce courts in no time at all. I don't like Alice, but I should have never let her drink that wine."

"Better Bill finds out what she's really like now instead of later," said John. "Hurry up and help me, Agatha. It's getting cold."

The sun had turned red and was low on the horizon. They

loaded up the trailer with the remainder of the plastic cups, the glasses, the punch-bowl, and then the table itself. As they drove out of the field, Agatha said, "I should have told Bill as well about Brent and his wife."

"I really don't think they had anything to do with it, Agatha."

"Someone had. Someone somewhere. Someone who could have been at this very fête."

They drove to the church hall first and carried the table in. There was still plenty of wine, stacked in boxes. "Just as well we didn't take the whole lot along," said John. "Where did you get the punch-bowl from?"

"I bought it."

"No one could call you mean, Agatha Raisin. It must have cost you a lot, what with the silver cups and all."

"Just doing my bit," said Agatha wearily.

"Will Bill book the Morris dancers?"

"No, I think he'll give them a warning and tell them not to dare drive until they've sobered up."

"That's all right. They'd hired a minibus. As long as the bus driver didn't have any of the wine, they'll be all right."

"We'll leave the cups and glasses here," said Agatha. "They can be used another time. I was too upset to notice. I hope the press had all gone by the time the dancers started fighting."

"Sorry. There was at least one television camera in action and I saw two press photographers."

"Damn."

"Let's go to my place and have a drink."

"No, mine," said Agatha. "I want to let my cats out."

After they had finished their drinks, they counted out the money on the kitchen table. "Nearly one hundred and fifty pounds, and that for the wine alone," said John. "Not bad. There must have been about only two boxes of wine left for them to steal."

"Miss Jellop must have brought most of the wine down here with her when she moved. It must have taken years to make a cellar-full of the stuff," said Agatha. "Let's take this money along to Mrs. Bloxby. She could raise a lot of money for the church with the wine that's left. But I think someone in the village who knows about home-made wine should figure out how to weaken it before any more is sold. At least that should be the end of Alice. I never could figure out what Bill saw in her."

"Maybe she's good in bed."

Agatha shuddered. For some reason she did not want to imagine Bill Wong in bed with anyone, least of all Alice.

Mrs. Bloxby welcomed them at the vicarage and took the bag of money from John. "I'll give this to Alf. He's in his study counting out the takings. From the initial look of things, we've done very well. It is all thanks to you, Agatha, and Alf is going to say so in his sermon next Sunday. I saw you talking to old Mrs. Feathers. Did she have anything interesting to say?"

"I should have spoken to her before," said Agatha. "She said she was sure Tristan had a mobile phone."

"And how does that help?"

"Because Mrs. Feathers said he had no calls the night after I left. But if, say, he had a mobile in his bedroom, someone could have rung him up and threatened him. He could have decided to flee and decided at the same time to take the church takings with him. He was too mean, I think, to let Mrs. Feathers know he had a phone of his own. He preferred to run up bills on hers."

"Did you tell Bill?"

"Yes, for once, I did. He's getting the police to check it."

"If only, oh, if only these murders could be solved."

"If they ever are," said Agatha, "I'll never complain of being bored again. But Bill has definitely warned me off for the last time, so I'll need to leave it to the police."

"He didn't warn me off," John pointed out.

But Agatha didn't like the idea of John playing detective when she herself was not allowed to.

"Mind you," she said, "there would be no harm in continuing to ask around the village. Look at the news I got from Mrs. Feathers. Might do no harm to go and talk to Mr. Crinsted, the man Tristan used to play chess with."

"I'll come with you," said John. "We'll try him in the morning."

"What do you know of Mark Brent?" Agatha asked Mrs. Bloxby.

"Nothing bad. Nice man. Always willing to help out. Why?"

"He was upset with Tristan. Seems his wife, Gladys, got a crush on Tristan and Brent warned him off."

"I cannot imagine for a moment that such as Mr. Brent or his wife would resort to violence of any kind," said Mrs. Bloxby.

"Well, we'll try Mr. Crinsted. Oh, and the mobile library is due round during the week. I'll have a word with Mrs. Brown."

"Do you think it will do any good?" asked the vicar's wife wearily.

Agatha could feel a resurgence of her old energy for investigation which had so recently deserted her. "I've blundered around asking questions before. Something's got to break."

Agatha and John drove to the council estate on Monday morning. "Do you think he'll be at home?" asked John.

"He's very old," replied Agatha. "Bound to be."

Mr. Crinsted answered the door to them. He was stooped and frail with a thin, lined face and mild eyes behind thick glasses. "Do come in," he said. "Dear me, how nice to have some company. The only company I usually have is the television set."

His living-room was neat and clean. Agatha looked at photographs on the mantelpiece of couples with children.

"How many children do you have?" she asked.

"A son and daughter and six grandchildren."

"Must be nice for you when they come on a visit."

"I'm afraid I only see them at Christmas. I think they find visits to me rather boring. The children are dreadfully spoilt."

How awful, thought Agatha, to be trapped here, never seeing anyone. Her mind worked busily. She would suggest to Mrs. Bloxby that they start an old folks' club.. Her stocks and shares had been doing very well. Maybe she could see about getting the church hall renovated, turn it into an old folks' club.

"The reason we called," said John, "is to ask you for your opinion of Tristan Delon."

"Oh dear. Do sit down. I'll make some tea."

Agatha glanced at her watch. "Don't worry. It's nearly lunch-time. Tell you what, we'll chat for a bit and then we'll go down to Moreton for some lunch. My treat."

John stared at Agatha in surprise, but Mr. Crinsted was obviously delighted. "Goodness me, it does seem an age since I've been out of the village. So what can I tell you about our late curate? Well, he called round one day when I was working out some chess moves and offered to play. I was so delighted to have a partner that I let him win on a couple of occasions. He was such good company. I thought he really liked me and that was very flattering to an old man like me. Then the last time, I became absorbed in the game and forgot to let him win. I have never in my life before seen anyone change personality so completely. He accused me of cheating. I patiently began to explain to him the moves I had made and he said, 'You're lying, you silly old fool,' and he upset the chessboard and sent the pieces flying and stalked out of the house. I was very disappointed. You see, I did think we might be friends."

"Before he became upset with you," said John, "did he let fall anything about his private life?"

"Not really. Chess is such a *silent* game. He did say once that people were like chess pieces, easily moved around. I pointed out that people could be very unpredictable."

"Let's continue this over lunch," said Agatha.

They went to a pub in Moreton and ate great helpings of steak-and-kidney pie. Agatha ordered wine. To John's amazement, she sparkled for Mr. Crinsted's benefit, telling him stories about her public relations jobs. Warmed by the wine and food, Mr. Crinsted talked in turn about his own life. He had been a nuclear physicist, working at Los Alamos, and then in Vienna. He had married an Austrian wife, Gerda, but she had died of breast cancer after their second child was born. "I spent a lot of money sending my son and daughter to the best schools and then university. Freda, my daughter, became a nurse and then married a doctor, and my son, Gerald, he became an accountant and married his secretary." Mr. Crinsted sighed. "I never saved any money and I was lucky to get that council house. I have a comfortable pension and my needs are small. I am glad both my children are very comfortably off."

"Don't they help you out?" asked John.

"I never ask them. I don't have any expensive needs. Perhaps I did too much for them and taught them to be selfish."

"You know the church hall?" asked Agatha.

"I know where it is, but that's all."

"I thought I might see about getting it repaired. The roof needs doing. I could start an old folks' club—films, bingo, stuff like that. You could give chess lessons. We'd need a minibus, too, to take people to the shops in Stratford, maybe the theatre."

"That would be wonderful. I would love to give chess lessons."

Again John looked at Agatha in surprise. He had recently come to think of her as a bossy, occasionally grumpy woman. But her eyes were sparkling with enthusiasm and old Mr. Crinsted looked positively rejuvenated.

He had to remind her after two hours of conversation that if they didn't hurry up, they would miss the mobile library.

After they had left Mr. Crinsted, John said, "Are you really going ahead with this old folks' club?"

"Yes, it'll be fun to have something to do."

"You surprise me."

"I can believe that. You have me down as a pushy, selfish woman."

"I have not," said John, reddening.

"There's the mobile library. Let's see what Mrs. Brown has to say."

They had to wait patiently while various villagers returned books, took out more books, and discussed books. At last they were left alone with Mrs. Brown.

"Mr. Delon?" Mrs. Brown looked at them thoughtfully over her half-moon glasses. "Now there was a young man just waiting to be murdered."

"Why do you say that?" asked John.

The plump little librarian picked a book off her desk and put it back on the shelves. "I've often thought about the way he humiliated me, jeering at my choice of books. There was no reason for it. It was an exercise in spite. I thought after I'd heard he had been murdered that if he could be bothered to go out of his way to be nasty to a country librarian, then he had probably been extremely nasty to someone who was prepared to retaliate."

"And you can think of no reason why he should suddenly have sounded off at you?" asked Agatha.

"There was one silly little thing. Mrs. Feathers likes romances, so I always choose one of the more innocent ones and keep it for her. She doesn't like the ones with explicit sex. We got talking one day and she said that Mr. Delon wanted to invest her savings for her. I told her that she should hang on to them, Mr. Delon was not a stockbroker. Perhaps that was what made him angry. But when Mrs. Feathers thanked me for my advice, I asked her not to tell Mr. Delon it came from me and she promised me she wouldn't tell him. That is why I thought his malice was unprompted."

"I think she probably did tell him," said Agatha. "What's the gossip about these murders?"

"I'm afraid a lot of people still suspect the vicar. They say Mr. Delon was murdered in the vicarage and that Miss Jellop and Mrs. Slither may have known something incriminating and Mr. Bloxby might have silenced them. It's ridiculous, I know, but frightened people do talk such rubbish and people *are* frightened. I see the duck races made the front page of the *Daily Bugle*."

"I haven't seen the papers today," said Agatha. "Have you got a copy?"

"Yes, I've one in my desk." Mrs. Brown pulled open a drawer. "Here it is."

There was a coloured photograph of the Morris men fighting. The headline read: THE PEACE OF THE ENGLISH COUNTRYSIDE. "Oh dear," said Agatha. "Never mind. We raised quite a bit of money."

There was nothing more about Tristan to be got from Mrs. Brown. "Two more dead ends," said John when he dropped Agatha off at her cottage. "Now what?"

"I'm going back to see Mrs. Bloxby," said Agatha. "I'm going to put forward my idea for the old folks' club."

"You're on your own, then. Maybe see you tomorrow."

"Yes, maybe," said Agatha vaguely, her mind full of plans.

"It really is too generous of you, Mrs. Raisin," said Mrs. Bloxby. "But what about all that wine? We'll need to find a new home for it."

"I've had an idea about that," said Agatha. "The wine is very heavy and sweet. We could relabel it and call it Cotswold Liqueur. I could ask John Fletcher if he would buy the wine. He could sell it by the glass as a liqueur. I could get a write-up on it in the local paper, do a bit of promotion in return. Tell him the proceeds will go to the old folks' home."

"That's a brilliant idea. I don't think all your money should go into the repairs. Now we have done so well for Save the Children, I think we should organize the next fund-raising venture to go to repairing the hall."

"I'll think of something good," said Agatha confidently.

"I am so glad to see you looking like your old self," said Mrs. Bloxby.

"I think I've finally got fed up with suffering over James. I'm going to have fun."

Agatha was hungry when she got home. Once more she scrabbled in the deep-freeze, scraping frost off labels in her search for something to eat. She was so tired, she did not notice that the tray of faggots she placed in the microwave was on a foil dish. She had not read the instructions properly and so did not know that foil was deemed unsuitable for microwaves. She had only read the time by dint of screwing up her eyes. Agatha should have realized that forty-five minutes in a microwave is a long time. While the dish spun round, she went into the garden and took a deep breath of the cold night air.

Was the murderer somewhere in the village? Was it possible to sleep easy at night after having committed three murders? As she stood there, lost in thought, she finally became aware of the frantic mewing of her cats and turned round. Black smoke was billowing out through the open kitchen door.

She rushed in. Flames were beginning to lick around the inside of the microwave. She switched it off and unplugged it and opened the door, coughing and waving her arms to try to clear the smoke. The foil tray had melted under a congealed black heap of food. Agatha lifted up the microwave and put it outside the kitchen door.

She found some slightly hard bread and cut two slices and toasted them with cheese under the grill. A film of black was lying over all the surfaces in the kitchen. When she had finished eating, she began to clean the kitchen. It was nearly midnight by the time she had finished.

Agatha went upstairs and had a hot bath and then changed into a long cotton night-dress. She climbed into bed and settled down with a weary sigh. What a day! At least the duck races had raised a lot of money. Pity about the bad publicity. So Bunty was married. She had achieved the dream of many secretaries by marrying the boss. Agatha's thoughts drifted back to the days when she herself had been a secretary. Her boss, an advertising manager, had been tall and blond and charming. Agatha had slavishly spent some of her small pay packet on buying special brands of coffee to please him. But he had never seemed to pay any more attention to her than if she were some sort of piece of office machinery. Mr. Crinsted's son had married his secretary.

She sat up, her mind racing. Miss Partle, Binser's secretary. What if she was so in love with her boss that she would defend him every way she could?

# TEN

†

WITHOUT even bothering to put on a dressing-gown, Agatha fled down the stairs, out into the night, straight to John's cottage and rang the bell and then hammered on the door.

"I'm coming," she heard John's cross voice shouting. He opened the door and stared at Agatha in her night-gown.

"Why, Agatha, this is so sudden."

"Don't be silly," said Agatha. "I've just got to talk to you."

He stood back and she walked into his living-room. John was bare-chested, wearing only a pair of blue silk pyjama trousers. His smooth chest was strong and muscled. Agatha wondered briefly what he did to keep so fit before plunging in. "Secretaries," she gasped.

"Sit down. Calm down. Begin at the beginning."

"I met my former secretary, Bunty, at the duck races. She'd married her boss. Mad about him."

"That's nice," said John soothingly. "But why come dashing in here in the middle of the night?"

"I just remembered how secretaries can obsess about their bosses. What about Miss Partle?"

"Binser's secretary?"

"Yes, her. Do you remember it was because of her that Binser met Tristan in the first place?"

"I think I do."

"Well, think of this. She could have been charmed by Tristan, enough to effect the introduction, but her real passion was for her boss. When Tristan conned Binser out of ten thousand, she must have been determined to get it back. She may have arranged to get him beaten up. So the ten thousand is returned. Still, Tristan tried a bit of blackmail. He loved money. He was desperate for money and more money. Miss Partle thought it was all over. But somehow Tristan gets his hands on a real piece of blackmail material concerning Binser. He phones Miss Partle. Say he speaks to her because Binser is away. She decides to silence him. She phones him in the middle of the night after you leave. Maybe she reminds Tristan of the beating in New Cross. He decides to make a break for it. He leaves the house and goes to the vicarage. She follows him quietly, not wanting to attack him in the street. Let's say he doesn't use his key to the vicarage but goes through the French windows. She sees him open the church box and take the money. She suddenly sees it would be to her advantage to get rid of him in such circumstances. She seizes the paper-knife, and bingo!"

"And what about Peggy Slither and Miss Jellop?"

"Tristan must have told them about what he had, or hinted at it. Miss Jellop, upset at his death, decides to phone Miss"

Partle. Maybe she thinks Miss Jellop knew more than she did; same with Peggy. She panics. Two more murders."

"Agatha, Agatha, think calmly. It's all too improbable. You're clutching at straws."

"Nevertheless, I am going up there tomorrow and I'm going to have a word with her and see her reaction. She can't do anything to me in a busy office."

John was about to point out that Binser's offices were in a quiet executive suite but restrained himself.

"Go back to bed," he said soothingly. "We'll talk about it tomorrow."

"Maybe I won't confront her right away," said Agatha. "I'll follow her after work, see where she lives, try to find out what sort of person she is."

"Yes, dear. Just go home," said John as if humouring a child.

"So you aren't coming with me?"

Unknown to Agatha, John had a dinner date for the following evening with Charlotte Bellinge, but he wasn't going to tell Agatha that. "I have a book to finish."

"Very well," said Agatha huffily. "I'll investigate on my own."

Agatha decided to be in London when Binser's offices closed for the night. That way she could follow Miss Partle, see where she lived, perhaps get some idea of her real character. She put on a disguise she had worn before of a blonde wig and spectacles with non-magnifying lenses.

Before she went, she was tempted to phone Bill, but then she remembered John's sheer disbelief at her deductions and realized Bill would probably feel the same.

Once at Binser's offices, she took one of the many seats in the large reception area, confident that no one would ask her what she was doing there. People came and went and the seats around her began to empty. Staff began to pour out of the building. The receptionists began to pack up for the night, their places being taken by two security guards. Agatha knew she was beginning to look conspicuous and so she left and lurked outside.

Time dragged on. A cold wind blew along Cheapside. Then suddenly Miss Partle appeared. Agatha sighed with relief. She had been worried that Miss Partle might be wearing a hat or something that might make her difficult to recognize. Keeping well behind her, Agatha followed Miss Partle along to St. Paul's tube and then down the long escalators to the Central Line platform. Now what to do? she wondered. Get into the same carriage? Why not, she decided. Miss Partle would not recognize her, disguised as she was.

They were travelling west. The carriage was crowded. Agatha straphung, peering occasionally through the press of bodies to where Miss Partle was standing, farther down the carriage.

The secretary got out at Notting Hill Gate and Agatha doggedly followed her. Miss Partle went quickly along Pembridge Road and to Agatha's disappointment went into a Turkish restaurant. Still, I'm disguised and I may as well eat something, thought Agatha. The restaurant was quiet. Agatha was placed three tables away from Miss Partle.

The secretary took the *Evening Standard* out of her briefcase and began to read. Agatha ordered kebab and rice and a glass of house wine. The restaurant began to fill up. Finally Miss Partle finished eating and reading and called for her bill. Agatha did the same. As Miss Partle was paying her bill, Agatha was overcome by a desire to pee. Cursing, she dived down the stairs to the toilet. When she emerged upstairs again, it was to find Miss Partle gone. Agatha paid her bill and rushed out into the night, looking to right and left. She saw the figure of Miss Partle turning left into Chepstow Villas and set off in pursuit. She paused at the end of the street and looked along. The sturdy figure of Miss Partle moved from pool of lamplight to pool of lamplight. Apart from a woman walking her dog, the street was empty. Then Agatha saw Miss Partle turn in at the gate of one of the early-Victorian houses. It had a holly tree at the gate. Agatha waited and then walked slowly along and once outside looked up at the house, wondering what to do next. She had learned nothing. Miss Partle had met no one, talked to no one. Agatha knew as little about her as she had always done.

She missed John. She missed someone to talk to. She took a notebook out of her handbag and made a note of the address. Perhaps she should check into a hotel for the night and try again the next day. Try what? jeered a voice in her head.

The more Agatha stood there and thought about Miss Partle being the killer, the more ridiculous it began to seem.

She decided to go home. After all, she hadn't told Doris Simpson to look after her cats. She had left dried food out for them, which her spoilt cats hated. No, it was time to go home and leave it all to the police.

John Armitage had endured a humiliating evening. He had arranged to meet Charlotte in a smart restaurant in the Kings Road. Charlotte had turned up half an hour late accompanied by a handsome young man. "This is Giles," she said. "Giles, John Armitage. You don't mind if Giles joins us, do you, darling?"

So John, who had hoped for a romantic evening, was forced to entertain Giles as well as Charlotte, and Giles was a man of few words. Apart from saying he thought reading books was a waste of time, he drank a lot and said little else. John began to hope that when the meal was over, maybe Charlotte would get rid of this boring young man and invite him home.

The price of the meal made him blink, but ever hopeful, he paid up. To his chagrin, once outside the restaurant, Charlotte thanked him firmly but sweetly for dinner, tucked her arm in Giles's and walked off with him down the Kings Road in the direction of her home.

John cursed himself for a fool. He found himself missing Agatha. He would have been better off to have gone with her on whatever mad-goose chase she was on. Agatha could be infuriating and bossy, but she was never boring. He had tried to discuss the case with Charlotte until he realized her beautiful eyes were glazing over with boredom. Charlotte, when not talking about herself, only liked to hear things she was interested in, like which restaurant or fashion designer was in and which was out.

The lights were out in Agatha's cottage when he arrived home. He decided that on the following day he would drive to Mircester where there was an excellent butcher and buy some steak and invite Agatha for dinner.

Agatha awoke the next day with the beginning of a sniffle. She was afraid she must have caught a cold with all that hanging around Cheapside in the cold wind. But somehow her belief that the murderer might be Miss Partle was renewed. She paced up and down her kitchen. Perhaps the thing she should have done was simply to confront the woman and see if she betrayed herself in any way.

Determination rose in her. She swept the morning's mail off the mat, including a note from John inviting her for dinner, and placed it on the hall table without looking at any of it. She served her cats chopped lambs' liver and then put a warm coat on and made her way out to her car.

In London, she parked her car in the underground car-park at Hyde Park and took the tube to Notting Hill Gate. The area was crowded as people made their way to the antiques market in the Portobello Road.

Agatha went straight to the house in Chepstow Villas and rang the bell and waited. There was no reply. She stood for a moment, irresolute, and then decided to take a look at the stalls in the Portobello Market. It felt odd to be surrounded once more by the smells and crowds of London. Agatha walked from stall to stall, examining jewellery, military badges and old clothes. She saw a handsome silver paper-knife and decided to buy it for Alf Bloxby. He would need a new one. The stall owner wrapped it up in tissue paper and Agatha slid it into her coat pocket.

She was just making her way through the crowds, past a man with a hurdy-gurdy and with a parrot on his shoulder when a voice in her ear said, "Mrs. Raisin?"

Agatha swung round. There was Miss Partle, surveying her.

"What a surprise!" said Agatha. "Isn't this market fascinating?"

"It is, if you can tell fake from genuine. But I like looking," said Miss Partle. "Like a coffee?"

"Thanks," said Agatha. "Where shall we go? It's so long since I've been here."

"I live close by. I was just going home."

They walked together chatting amiably about how London had changed and all the while Agatha was thinking, I must have been mad to suspect this nice woman.

In Chepstow Villas, Miss Partle unlocked the door. Agatha followed her into a sitting-room which led off a narrow entrance corridor. It was furnished with good antiques and some fine paintings. The room, which had originally consisted of front and back parlours, was now one long room with long windows front and back.

Miss Partle went to a thermostat on the wall and turned it up. "Keep your coat on. It's chilly in here but it will soon warm up. Come downstairs to the kitchen and I'll make coffee."

"This is a fine house," said Agatha when they were downstairs, looking around the gleaming modern kitchen. "You've put a lot of work into it."

"I bought it with an inheritance from an aunt back when Notting Hill was still pretty unfashionable and got work done on it every time I could afford it. Take a seat and tell me why you were following me yesterday in that strange disguise. The coffee will be ready in a minute."

Agatha laughed. "You are never going to believe this. I must have had a rush of blood to the head. I didn't know you had spotted me last night."

"That's a very distinctive ring you are wearing. You should have left it off. And the wind must have disarranged your wig. I noticed in the restaurant that a strand of brown hair had escaped. I studied you when you thought I wasn't looking and finally I was able to place you and then I saw you standing outside my house. So what were you doing?"

"I may as well tell you. I hope you are not going to be too furious with me. It all started at the duck races."

"This sounds weird. Duck races? What has that got to do with me? Oh, the coffee is ready. How do you take it?"

"Just black. Do you mind if I smoke?"

"Yes, I do."

"I'll live without one."

"Here's your coffee. Now tell me why you were following me."

"Well, at these duck races in the village, I met my former secretary, Bunty, who had married her boss. I got to thinking about secretaries who were in love with their bosses and I thought that if Mr. Binser had been under some sort of threat from Tristan, you might have stepped in to protect him. It all seems fantastic now I'm here talking to you."

"I should be angry but I suppose three murders in and around your village must have made you want to grasp at straws. So the police have no leads?"

"Not unless the one I've just given them comes to anything."

"And what was that?"

"Mrs. Feathers, the elderly lady Tristan was living with, she told me she had once seen him using a mobile phone. I told the police. You see, he might have got a phone call on the night he died that frightened him. I think he broke into the church box to take the money because he planned to make a run for it and wanted some petty cash. So if there was a call, they'll be able to trace who it was."

A cloud crossed the sun, darkening the garden outside, where two starlings pecked for worms in the small lawn.

"You don't see many of them nowadays," said Agatha.

"What? Mobile phones?"

"No, starlings. London used to be full of them. I was looking at the starlings on your lawn."

"Tell me about these duck races," said Miss Partle. "It sounds very primitive. It's a wonder you didn't have the animal-rights people after you or the Royal Society for the Protection of Birds."

"These were plastic ducks, the little yellow ones." Agatha told her all about the races and the drunken Morris men.

"I didn't realize there was so much fun to be had in a village," said Miss Partle. "What on earth made you decide to poke around in murder?"

"Insatiable curiosity, I guess. But I have no intention of giving up until I find out who did it."

"Well, you know what they say: curiosity killed the cat. Would you like to see the rest of the house?"

"Not really," said Agatha. "I think I'd better be getting back down to the country."

"You were talking about all that wine the dead woman's sister gave to the races. I've built up quite a cellar. Not home-made, mind. Good stuff."

"You have a cellar?"

"Yes, here." Miss Partle opened a door in the kitchen. "Come on. You can choose a bottle."

Agatha walked to the cellar door and peered down some stone steps. "You go on down," said Miss Partle behind her. "I'll just switch off the percolator."

"Is there a light switch?" said Agatha, uneasily reminded of being trapped in Mrs. Tremp's coal cellar.

"On the inside of the door on your right." Agatha was searching inside the door for the switch when a massive blow struck her on the back of the head and she fell headlong down the steps and lay in a heap at the bottom.

Agatha could feel pain all over though she was still conscious, but as she heard Miss Partle coming down the stairs, with what was left of her wits she realized she had better look as if she were unconscious.

Then she felt her ankles being bound and then her wrists. A piece of strong adhesive tape was put over her mouth. "Interfering bitch," hissed Miss Partle. "I thought that phone had been got rid of. I phoned from a call-box round the corner. I hope they don't realize the phone-box is near where I live. What'll I do now? I'll be back. Oh, God, why couldn't you leave things alone!"

Agatha heard her footsteps mounting the stairs and then the cellar door banged shut. At first Agatha was in such a state of pain and fright that her brain did not seem to be able to work at all. Then she thought dismally that she should have told Bill her suspicions. When she went missing, John would tell him, and he would then question Miss Partle and maybe her body would be found.

John Armitage carried his groceries to his car parked in the public car-park in front of Mircester police headquarters. Bill Wong hailed him. "On your own? Where's your fiancée?"

For one split second, John wondered whom he was taking about and then rallied and said, "Oh, Agatha. She must still be up in London. Any luck with that mobile phone?"

"There was a call to him the night he was murdered. It came from a call-box in Notting Hill."

"Pity. Look, Bill, I hope she isn't getting herself into trouble."

"You'd better tell me."

"It's just that she had this mad idea that the murderer was Miss Partle—you know, Binser's secretary."

"Why on earth should she think that?"

"It's because she met her former secretary at the duck races. Former secretary married her boss. Agatha starts thinking about secretaries who are in love with their bosses and comes to the mad conclusion that the respectable Miss Partle must have gone around bumping off people to protect Binser. I just hope she doesn't get into trouble. She's gone to find out about her. Binser's got powerful friends."

Bill stood very still. "I've often thought," he said slowly, "that although Agatha might sometimes do silly things, she is possessed of an almost psychic ability to leap to the right conclusion."

John looked unconvinced. "Unless Miss Partle has any

connection with Notting Hill, the whole idea remains far-fetched."

"I have the addresses of everyone concerned with the murder cases in the station," said Bill. "Do no harm to have a look."

"I'll come with you."

"All right." Bill led the way into police headquarters and told John to take a seat and wait.

John waited and waited, feeling increasingly uneasy. Bill was taking an unusually long time.

At last Bill came out. "Miss Partle lives in Notting Hill," he said. "I've phoned Kensington to pull her in for questioning just in case, and hope Binser doesn't sue us."

"Give me the address," said John.

"No, one amateur is enough. Leave it to the police."

John raced to the post office and asked for the London phone directory. He located Miss Partle's address, got back into his car and set off at speed for London.

Agatha was in a state of sheer terror. For a long time she was unable to think. Then she remembered that paper-knife she had bought and put in the pocket of her coat. She twisted her bound hands, trying to get her fingers inside her coat pocket.

Then the cellar door opened again. This is it, thought Agatha. Miss Partle came down the stairs carrying a hammer. "I'll just put an end to you," she said, "and then worry about getting rid of the body later."

She hefted the hammer and Agatha closed her eyes. Then, above their heads, the doorbell shrilled.

Miss Partle lowered the hammer. Should she answer it or wait for them to go away? But sometimes Mr. Binser sent important documents to her home for her to study. She dropped the hammer on the floor beside Agatha and went back up the stairs.

She opened the street door. Two policemen stood there. "Miss Partle?"

"Yes?"

"I wonder if you would accompany us to the police station. Just a few more questions concerning the murder of Tristan Delon."

"But I have already answered all your questions. Mr. Binser will be most displeased."

"It won't take long."

The desire to get them away from the house prompted Miss Partle to say, "I'll fetch my handbag."

Agatha heard the voices but could not make out what they were saying. She heard Miss Partle go back into the kitchen, and then back to the front door. Agatha began to bang her feet on the floor. But the door slammed shut behind Miss Partle and the house was quiet.

Bill and Detective Chief Inspector Wilkes were speeding for London, siren blaring. "I told them to hold this Miss Partle until we got there," said Wilkes.

"I've been thinking," said Bill, "what if Agatha's gone to her house?"

"They say she seemed to be alone."

"Might be an idea to call at the house first and ask the neighbours if they saw anyone like Agatha call at the door. Only take a minute," he pleaded.

Wilkes sighed. "Well, all right. But I've got a feeling we'll have Binser's lawyers on top of us by the end of the day. Agatha Raisin. Pah! Why can't she mind her own business?"

"She's often blundered onto something in the past."

"If there's nothing in this, I'll charge that damn woman with interfering in police business and I really will do it this time!"

• • •

Down in the cellar, Agatha rolled onto her back again with a groan. Why wasn't real life like the movies? In a movie, the heroine would have been able to get her hands on that knife and free her bonds.

She lay still for a moment and tried again. Her pockets were deep. She got a finger on the edge of the tissue paper and gently tugged. Bit by bit the knife began to emerge from her pocket. She gave a final tug and the knife in its tissue-paper wrapping popped out and fell on the floor. She rolled on her side and felt for it. But the tissue-paper wrapping had been Sellotaped around the knife and she could not get enough movement in her fingers to tear it off. Tears began to roll down her cheeks.

John Armitage was caught up in a traffic jam. He heard the sound of a police siren and saw the cars in front twist to the side of the road. A police car roared past. He got a glimpse of Bill Wong's face. He suddenly felt that Agatha had made a terrible mistake and the police would never forgive her.

"This is the house," said Bill. "Let's try next door and find out if Agatha's been seen."

A young woman with two children hanging on her skirts opened the door. Bill described Agatha. She shook her head. "I've been busy with the children. Ask old Mrs. Wirtle across the street. She never misses anything."

Mrs. Wirtle took ages to answer the door. She was leaning on a zimmer frame, peering up at them from under a bird's nest of uncombed grey hair. Once more, Bill described Agatha.

"Yes, I saw a woman like that go in with Miss Partle," said Mrs. Wirtle. "Then Miss Partle was taken away by the police. What's going on?"

"And you did not see the other woman come out?" demanded Bill in a loud voice.

"No need to shout. I'm not deaf. No, I didn't see her."

They thanked her and went and stood in front of Miss Partle's house. "Might take too long to get a search warrant," said Wilkes.

"Try the door," suggested Bill.

Wilkes turned the handle. "It's open."

"Then we can go in," said Bill. "Responsible policemen checking unlocked premises."

Agatha heard men's voices. Had Miss Partle associates? But she was desperate. She made choking noises behind her gag and banged her feet on the floor.

"You hear something?" asked Bill, as they stood in the narrow entrance corridor.

They stood and listened. Again a faint banging sound followed by a moan.

They walked down to the kitchen. "Agatha!" called Bill sharply.

A stifled gurgling moan.

"That door over there is open," said Bill.

He fumbled inside the door and located the light switch and pressed down.

There down on the cellar floor lay Agatha Raisin, her face blotched with tears.

The two men hurried down. Bill ripped the gag from her mouth and then, producing a clasp knife, cut the ropes that bound her.

"She was going to kill me," gasped Agatha. "She's coming back to kill me."

Bill helped her to her feet. Agatha staggered and winced at the pain in her feet and hands, for the ropes had nearly cut off her circulation.

"Get her upstairs and give her some tea," said Wilkes. "I'll phone Kensington. They've got Miss Partle there."

The Kensington police were becoming increasingly worried. This Miss Partle was formidable and business-like. She seemed to have powerful friends and her boss was a tycoon.

Miss Partle sensed their unease and was becoming increasingly confident. All she had to do was sit tight and sooner or later they would release her. She was not under arrest. All she had to do was answer the questions put to her by the clowns from Mircester police, go home, and decide what to do with Agatha Raisin's body. If she and Agatha had been spotted together at the market, then she might have more questions to answer, but so long as there was no body to be found, there was not much they could do. It might be an idea to put the body in the boot of her car and dump it somewhere in Carsely.

A policewoman had been sitting with her. But the door of the interview room opened and two detectives came in. They looked at her grimly. One said, "We'll start the questioning when Detective Chief Inspector Wilkes of the Mircester CID arrives."

It was then that Miss Partle realized she could not remember locking her front door.

John Armitage arrived just as Bill and Wilkes were ushering Agatha into their police car.

"Come with us," said Bill, "and look after your fiancée. She was nearly killed."

As they drove to the police station, Agatha told her story.

"I wonder why she attacked you?" said John when Agatha had finished. "I mean, you didn't say anything that might lead her to think you had any proof at all, did you?"

Agatha shook her head. "Mind you, I did tell her about

the mobile phone and I did say I would never give up trying to find out who did it." She was beginning to recover. The old Agatha Raisin was coming back. And the old Agatha Raisin was thinking what a pill John was. No glad hugs or kisses. No cries of "Darling, are you all right?" Sod him.

At the police station, John was told to wait while Agatha was led off by a detective to give her statement.

Bill and Wilkes entered the interview room where Miss Partle was sitting.

Wilkes said, "I am charging you with the attempted murder of Mrs. Agatha Raisin . . ."

And Miss Partle began to scream.

# ELEVEN

✝

BILL began to think she had gone mad and that they were never going to get a coherent statement out of her, but at last she calmed and it all came out.

"I am devoted to my boss," she said in a flat, even voice. "I did everything for him, more than his wife. I made him the best coffee, I put his shirts in the laundry, I bought the Christmas and birthday presents for his children as well as dealing with his business affairs. Then I received a message one day to say there was a Mr. Tristan Delon in reception. He wished to see Mr. Binser with a view to getting a charitable donation towards a boys' club. I sent down a message that he should put his request in writing."

Wilkes occasionally interrupted to ask for times and dates.

"He must have somehow got a description of me from one

of the receptionists, for when I left that evening, he was waiting for me. He invited me for dinner. He was very charming and I knew that Mr. Binser would never love me the way I wanted him to, and it was like a perpetual ache at my heart. Tristan made me feel attractive. I found myself promising him an interview with my boss. And then suddenly Mr. Binser and Tristan seemed to be going everywhere, but Tristan was still careful to take me out as well from time to time.

"Then Mr. Binser came to me and told me how he had been cheated out of ten thousand pounds. I told Tristan to visit me at my home. I took a cricket bat to him and said that was only a taste of what he would get if he didn't return the money, and I thought that was the end of it. I checked with his vicar and found he had moved to the country.

"And then, when I had all but forgotten about him, he phoned me. He said he and Mr. Binser had gone to a gay bar and a friend who worked there had sent pictures of Tristan and Mr. Binser. Tristan said to tell Mr. Binser that if he did not pay up two hundred and fifty thousand, the photographs would go to his wife. Much as I thought Mr. Binser's wife was not worthy of him, I knew he would be devastated. I hated Tristan Delon. He had fooled me. He had let me think he cared for me. I went down to Carsely in disguise, dressed as a rambler. I saw a group of ramblers and tagged on to them until I got a plan of the village in my head. I was still thinking what to do. You see, I told him I had money saved and I would pay him the money myself. I watched and waited. I saw that Raisin woman leave his house around midnight. And then I wondered if I could frighten him into leaving. So I phoned him and told him I would call on him the following day and I would shoot him. You see, I was beginning to wonder if there really were any photographs. Because I'd asked my boss if he'd ever been to a gay bar and he said he hadn't, and Mr. Binser," she said, all mad pride, "*never* lies.

"Tristan did sound frightened. But I waited. I saw him slip out and walk to the vicarage. He entered by the French windows. I slipped in after him. I saw him open a box and take money out and at the same time I saw the paper-knife, gleaming in the moonlight. I seized it and stabbed him and left. I had parked my car among woods at the top of the hill and I made my way across the fields to it."

She fell silent.

"Miss Jellop?" prompted Wilkes. "Why her?"

"Tristan had told her. She said he had left the photos with a Mrs. Slither but that she, Miss Jellop, knew all about it. She said he had got drunk one day and told her. She said she was going to the police. She said she was up in London and calling from a phone-box. I couldn't have that. I said I would call on her and give her a full explanation. I was so lucky to get to her first. But would it never end? Then I had that Slither woman saying she was sure Tristan had told her that he had enough evidence to ruin Mr. Binser. I hoped it was over but then I began to worry about Peggy Slither. Getting rid of her would make sure there would be an end to it. I carefully looked through her house after I had killed her without disturbing anything, but could not see any photographs. I waited and prayed, but it became evident that the police had not found any either. You won't tell Mr. Binser about any of this? I would not want to lose his respect."

"I'm afraid we'll have to," said Wilkes and Miss Partle began to cry.

Agatha, for the next few weeks, was frightened into domesticity. Doris Simpson, her cleaner, had gone on holiday to Spain, leaving Agatha to look after her cat, Scrabble. Agatha had brought back Scrabble from one of her cases, had *rescued* Scrabble, but the ungrateful cat seemed to be pining for the missing Doris, and did not appear to remember Agatha at all. Agatha polished and cleaned and had a brave try at making apple jelly from a basket of windfall apples which Farmer Brent had given her but it would not set, so she gave the jars of runny liquid to Mrs. Bloxby, who miraculously did something to them to turn them into golden jelly.

The vicar, Alf Bloxby, had called in person to thank Agatha for her help. He made such a polite and formal speech that Agatha wryly thought that his wife had coached him in what to say.

John Armitage was often up in London and she saw little of him.

Then Bill Wong called round to tell Agatha that Miss Partle had gone completely mad and it was doubtful if she would ever stand trial.

"It was a visit from Binser that seems to have sent her over the edge," said Bill. "He'd got her the best lawyer, but she kept asking to see him. I don't know what was said, but after his visit, they had to put her in a strait-jacket. One always thinks of romantic people as suffering from undying passion, not plain, middle-aged secretaries."

"Those gay photographs that Wilkes told me about, had Binser known anything about them?"

"No, evidently all he remembers is her asking him if he'd ever gone to a gay bar, and he was surprised, said no, and asked her why. She had responded with something non-committal. As for Jellop and Slither, their end was partly your fault, Agatha."

"How come?"

"I think both of them were jealous of you and wanted to show they could be detectives as well. It's very dangerous to keep things from the police. You should have told me about your suspicions, not gone to see her yourself. I mean, what on earth were you thinking of, going back with her to her house?"

"It was when I met her in the Portobello Market," said Agatha. "She seemed so normal that I decided I must have been fantasizing."

"But it was a leap in the dark to suspect her."

"It was this secretary business," said Agatha. "I was a secretary once. People think because of women's lib that secretaries no longer make the coffee or things like that. But the top-flight go on more like wives. Some of them even choose schools for the boss's children. There's an intimacy springs up. Often boss and secretary work together late. Men like to talk about their work and secretaries make good listeners while wives at home get bored with it all. He probably saw Miss Partle as a cross between mother and helper. And she probably lived on romantic dreams of him. Tristan must have provided a brief holiday from her obsession until she found out that he had been using her. Then all her passion for Binser would return and engulf her."

Bill's eyes were shrewd. "You sound as if you're speaking from personal experience."

"No, just speculation. How's Alice?"

"She's fine."

"I thought after that scene at the duck races that it would all be over."

"She was drunk. She cried so hard and apologized so sincerely that I was quite touched."

"You're touched in the head," said Agatha acidly.

"What's that supposed to mean?"

"Bill, trust me, Alice is one cast-iron bitch. She wants to get married and with that mouth of hers, I doubt if anyone else would have her."

Bill stood up and jerked on his coat. "Just because you've

been crossed in love, Agatha, you see the worst in anyone else's romance. You should be ashamed of yourself. Who I see or what I do is none of your business."

"But, Bill . . ." wailed Agatha.

"I'm off."

After he had gone, Agatha sat feeling miserable. If she wanted to retain his friendship, she would need to apologize to him. But what on earth did he see in the awful Alice?

Restless, she looked around her gleaming cottage. Better to get started on the old folks' club and take her mind off things.

She walked along to the vicarage. Mrs. Bloxby was out in the garden planting winter pansies.

"You look upset, Mrs. Raisin," she said, straightening up from a flower-bed. "It's not too cold today. I'll bring some coffee out into the garden so you can have a cigarette and you can tell me what's been going on."

When they were seated at the garden table with mugs of coffee, Mrs. Bloxby asked, "What's up?"

"It's Bill," said Agatha. "You'll never believe this. He's still devoted to Alice."

"And what's that got to do with you?"

"He's my friend and he's making a terrible mistake. I told him she was a cast-iron bitch."

"Oh, Mrs. Raisin, you cannot interfere in a relationship."

"Really? It was you who told me my marriage to James would be a disaster."

The vicar's wife looked rueful. "So I did. But I was so worried about you."

"As I am about Bill."

"True. But you'd better apologize. He is too good a friend to lose."

Agatha sighed. "I'm tired of blundering around other people's lives. I thought I would sound out some builders about getting the church-hall roof repaired for a start."

"I am so glad you are still going to go on with that. John Fletcher, at the pub, is going to take the wine and label it as a liqueur. He says half of the price of each glass sold will go to the new club."

"That's handsome of him. I'll make a push and try to get it all ready by Christmas. Have some sort of party."

"When is the trial?" asked Mrs. Bloxby.

"It seems as if there isn't going to be one. Miss Partle has lost her marbles and will be considered unfit to stand trial. You know, I had one thought when I was lying in that cellar—I haven't made a will. Maybe I'll leave it all to the church and go straight to heaven."

"You'll want to leave it to your husband."

"What husband?"

"I cannot imagine you staying single for the rest of your life."

Agatha grinned. "Maybe I'll marry John Armitage after all."

"There's not enough of a spark there."

"Does one need a spark at my age?"

"At any age."

"I'll think about it. I'll go home and phone around some builders."

Agatha went to feed her cats because their bowls were empty and she couldn't remember feeding them. I'm turning into a compulsive cat feeder, she thought as she poached fish for them and then set it aside to cool. She saw John's keys lying on the kitchen counter and decided to go next door and pick up his mail from the doormat and put it on his desk.

In his cottage, she scooped up the pile of post. She looked thoughtfully at his answering machine. Why all these trips to

London? Feeling guilty, she laid down the post on his desk and crossed to the answering machine. There were several messages, and all from Charlotte Bellinge. He must have saved them, thought Agatha dismally. The first one was Charlotte apologizing for bringing some man called Giles to dinner. "Do forgive me, dear John," she cooed. "Do let me take you out for dinner and make it up to you." The second said, "What a wonderful time we had. Pippa is giving a party tomorrow night. Do say you'll come." And the third, "I'm running a bit late. Can you pick me up at nine instead of eight? Dying to see you."

So that's that, thought Agatha. No heading into the sunset of middle age with John Armitage.

She went home and arranged the cooled fish in bowls for the cats. The loneliness of the cottage seemed to press down on her.

Agatha picked up the phone and dialled old Mr. Crinsted's number. "Feel like coming out for dinner?" she asked.

"Delighted," said the old man.

"I'll pick you up in half an hour," said Agatha.

Agatha found she was enjoying herself in Mr. Crinsted's company. They discussed plans for the old folks' club and Mr. Crinsted promised to teach Agatha chess.

"I am so glad you called, Mrs. Raisin," he said. "I wanted to hear all about the murders."

"I would have called earlier," lied Agatha, who had practically until that evening forgotten Mr. Crinsted's existence, "but I've been settling down after the shock of it all."

"Tell me about it, Mrs. Raisin."

"Agatha."

"Right, my name is Ralph."

So Agatha did while Ralph Crinsted listened intently. When she had finished, he said, "It's odd, all the same."

"What's odd?"

"This Miss Partle must have been so used to discussing everything with him, I'm surprised she decided to take matters into her own hands."

"I've met Binser. He's a straightforward man. He probably never noticed much about her. Thought of her as a bit of office machinery."

"I think any man who had a secretary so much in love with him would have noticed something."

"Maybe he did and took it as his due. Men do, you know."

"Some men."

"I'm just glad it's all over and Alf Bloxby is in the clear. Not that there was ever any evidence against him, but there was gossip, and gossip in a small village can be very dangerous."

"True. Have you ever played chess before?"

"No, never."

"Like to learn?"

"I wouldn't mind."

"Then I'll give you lessons."

After she had dropped Mr. Crinsted off at his home, Agatha reflected that it was a long time since she had enjoyed such a carefree evening.

She had promised to call on Ralph Crinsted in a couple of days' time and start her chess lessons. Then tomorrow, she would see what estimate the builders came up with for the roof. The ring on her finger sparkled. "Masquerade over," said Agatha ruefully to her cats. She took off the ring and put it in the kitchen drawer. She wondered how John was getting on with Charlotte and realized with relief that his relationship didn't bother her in the slightest. Or that was what she believed. Almost impossible to imagine John getting passionate about anyone. Like Miss Partle. Poor Miss Partle. Now why think that?

This was a woman who was a stone-cold murderess and who was probably faking insanity.

John Armitage was at another hot and noisy party in Chelsea with Charlotte flirting with a group of men across the room. But he could bear it. Tonight was going to be the night. Hadn't she said they would just drop in for an hour and then go home together? He remembered fondly the seductive look in her eyes when she had said those words and the caress in her voice.

He had been disappointed that she had still shown no interest in the murders except to laugh and say that Agatha Raisin was a formidable woman.

John looked at his watch, only half listening to the woman next to him, who was telling him that she was sure she could sit down and write a book if she only had the time. They had been there two hours and Charlotte showed no signs of leaving. Time to take charge. He crossed the room and took her arm in a possessive grip. "Time we were leaving."

"Oh, darling." Charlotte pouted prettily. "We're all going on to Jilly's party."

John did not know who this Jilly was and he did not care.

He said stiffly, "Either we leave now or I'm going home."

"Then you'd better go. But why not come with us? It'll be fun."

"Good night," snapped John.

As he strode to the door, he heard one of the men with Charlotte laugh and say, "There goes another of Charlotte's walkers."

His face flamed. That had been all she had really wanted from him, an escort to walk her to the endless social functions she loved.

His thoughts turned to Agatha on the road home. He had been neglecting her along with his work. He would get going on the book for a couple of days and then take her out for dinner. But, damn Charlotte Bellinge. She had really led him a fine dance.

Agatha was busy with the builders next day and with looking around the church hall. Old people like comfort and dignity. The floor would need a carpet and she would need to supply comfortable chairs and tables. Bookshelves along one wall for books, games and jigsaws. What else? The walls painted, of course, but not in those dreadful pink and pale-blue pastel colours do-gooders liked to inflict on the old as if catering for a second childhood. Plain white would do, with pictures. It should really be called the Agatha Raisin Club, considering all the work and money she was putting into it. But Mrs. Bloxby would think she was being grandiose. Of course, she had promised to think up some fund-raising venture so that she would not have to bear all the cost herself. Agatha's mind worked busily. An auction would be a good idea. She had raised a lot of money for one of those before by going around the country houses and getting them to contribute. Or what about getting some well-known pop group to put on a concert? No, scrub that. It would bring in too much mess and probably drugs as well. She must think of something.

She walked back to her cottage in the pouring rain, trying to avoid the puddles gathering amongst the fallen leaves.

In her cottage, there was a note lying on the kitchen table from Doris Simpson, one of the few women in Carsely to use Agatha's first name. "Dear Agatha," she read, "Have taken poor Scrabble home to feed. Cat looks half-starved. Be round to clean as usual next week. Doris."

"Bloody cat ate like a horse," muttered Agatha.

The doorbell rang. Agatha answered it. John stood there. He had suddenly decided he wanted to see Agatha.

"Yes?" asked Agatha coldly.

"Can I come in? It's bucketing with rain."

He followed her into the kitchen.

"So what were you doing in London?" asked Agatha.

"This and that. Bookshops, agent, publisher, the usual round. Are you free for dinner this evening?"

"I think I've got a date," lied Agatha. "I'll check."

She dialled Mr. Crinsted's number. "Is our date for tonight, Ralph, sweetie?" asked Agatha in a husky voice.

"I thought we'd arranged to play chess tomorrow," came the surprised voice at the other end. "But tonight, any time is fine."

"Look forward to it," said Agatha. "See you then." She put down the receiver and turned to John.

"Sorry, I've got a date."

"Well, what about tomorrow?"

"Sorry, going to be busy for some time." And I am not interested in Charlotte Bellinge's leavings, thought Agatha. She must have ditched him.

"I'll leave you to it." John marched out, feeling doubly rejected. The rain poured down. What am I doing stuck in this village? thought John angrily. It doesn't help a bit with the writing. I was better off in London.

After he had gone, Agatha took the ring he had given her out of the drawer and put it in an envelope. On her way out that evening, she popped it through his letter-box. Not that she was jealous of Charlotte Bellinge.

For Ralph Crinsted's sake, Agatha tried to concentrate on her chess lesson while privately wondering what could be the fun in playing such a boring game. There seemed to be so much to memorize. "I don't think you're going to make a chess player," said Ralph finally. "You're not enjoying this one bit."

"I will, I will," said Agatha. And with a rare burst of honesty, she added, "You see, I'm not used to concentrating on anything other than people—what motivates them, why they commit murder, that sort of thing. Let's try again another night. I'll buy some sort of book, *Chess Made Easy,* or something like that, so I'll be geared-up next time."

"If you say so. Do you play cards?"

"Don't know many games. Poker. I once played poker."

"Like a game?"

"Sure."

Agatha actually won the first game and began to enjoy herself. It had reached midnight when she finally put down the cards and said ruefully, "I'm keeping you up late."

"Doesn't matter. I don't sleep much. The old don't, you know."

As Agatha drove home, she thought with a shiver of impending old age and loneliness, would she endure white nights and long days? Would her joints seize up with arthritis?

Tomorrow, she thought gloomily, I'll draft out my will. I'm not immortal.

Had the weather cleared up, Agatha might have put off thoughts of making out a will, but another day of rain blurred the windows of her cottage and thudded down on the already rain-soaked garden.

She went into the sitting-room, carrying her cigarettes and a mug of coffee and sat down at her desk. She took a small tape recorder out of her drawer and had got as far as "This is the last will and testament of Mrs Agatha Raisin" when there was a ring at the doorbell.

"Blast," muttered Agatha and went to answer it.

Mr. Binser stood there. "Good heavens," said Agatha. "Come in out of this dreadful rain. What brings you?"

"I just came to see you and thank you for clearing up those dreadful murders," said the tycoon. "I'm curious. How did you arrive at the truth?"

Agatha took his coat and ushered him into the sitting-room. "Coffee?"

"No," he said, sitting down on the sofa. "I haven't much time. So how did you guess it was my Miss Partle?"

Agatha, glad of an opportunity to brag, told him how she had managed to leap to the conclusion that the culprit was Miss Partle.

"Interesting," he said when she had finished. "You seem such a confident lady. Are you never wrong?"

"I pride myself I'm not."

"You were certainly right about Miss Partle's adoration of me."

Agatha felt a lurch in her stomach. "You mean I was wrong about something else?"

"If there is one thing I hate, it is busy-body interfering women."

The rain drummed against the windows and dripped from the thatch outside. The day was growing darker. Agatha switched on a lamp next to her. "That's better," she said with a lightness she did not feel. "At least you don't go around killing them."

There was a long silence while Binser studied her. Agatha broke it by saying sharply, "I have a feeling you came to tell me something."

"Yes. You are so unbearably smug. You see, Miss Partle didn't commit these murders. I did."

Agatha goggled at him. "Why? How?"

"In all my life," he said calmly, "no one has ever managed to put one over on me—except Tristan Delon. I suppose, in my way, I was as infatuated with that young man as Miss Partle was with me. I married for money, the daughter of a wealthy company director. I never had any real friends. I felt I could be honest with Tristan, I could relax with him. Then he cheated me. All he had ever wanted from me was money. I hated him. I have certain underworld contacts which come in useful from time to time. I arranged to have him beaten up. I got Miss Partle to tell him who had done it. He returned the money and I thought that was that. But the leech wouldn't let go. He phoned Miss Partle and said he was going to tell my wife unless I paid up. I found he had gone to the country. I went down to Carsely. I had already studied ordnance survey maps of the area. I dressed as a rambler and left my car hidden some distance outside the village and crossed the fields so that I would get down to where he was living without being seen. I decided to give him one more chance. I had his mobile phone number. I phoned Miss Partle and told her to go out to the nearest phone-box and call him and tell him I was coming to kill him. I thought I would give him a chance to run for it.

"I hid behind one of the gravestones in the churchyard where I could watch the entrance to his cottage. The door is clearly illuminated by that one streetlight. I saw him slip out and head for the vicarage. I saw him enter by those French windows and followed him. There he stood in the moonlight like a fallen angel, rifling the contents of the church box. I saw that paper-knife. I was in such a blinding rage. I did not know it was so sharp. I drove it down into his neck.

"And then I ran. I told Miss Partle what I had done and she said that no one would ever suspect me. And then you came to see me. I thought I had shut you up with my statement to the police, and then I found myself being threatened by a village spinster called Jellop who Tristan had told about me. She said she felt she should go to the police with what she knew. She said Tristan had photographs of the pair of us in a gay bar. Now

Tristan had taken me to one once. I said I would call and see her and she was not to go to the police until I explained things. So that was the end of her. When Peggy Slither told me she actually had the photographs, I thought the nightmare would never end. I said I would pay her two hundred thousand for the photos and she agreed. I didn't trust her. She kept crowing about what a great detective she was. I felt she might take my money and tell the police all the same. After she had handed me the photographs and I had given her the money, she suddenly snatched back the photographs. 'This isn't right,' she said. 'I told someone I would go to the police and so I will.' I found out that she had not mentioned my name. I said mildly, 'All right, but what about a cup of tea?' What a triumphant bully she was. I followed her quietly into her kitchen and slid a carving knife out of the drawer. She turned just as I was raising the knife and screamed." He shrugged. "But it was too late."

Agatha felt cold sweat trickling down the back of her neck.

"I made an arrangement with Miss Partle that should anything break, she was to take the blame."

"But why should she do that?" demanded Agatha hoarsely while her frightened eyes roamed around the room looking for a weapon.

"I told her if she took the rap, with good behaviour she would be out in ten years' time and I would marry her. I knew she would go through hell if only I married her."

"Are you going to kill me?" asked Agatha.

"No, you silly cow, I am not. You have no proof. And poor Miss Partle is now stone-mad. You won't get anything out of her. If it hadn't been for you, she wouldn't be in prison. I couldn't bear the idea of you sitting smugly in your cottage thinking what a great detective you are."

"I'll tell the police!" panted Agatha.

"And what proof will they find? Nothing. You will find

that the police, having got her confession, will not thank you for trying to re-open the case. I have powerful friends. Goodbye, Mrs. Raisin."

Agatha sat very still. She heard the door slam. She heard him driving off. She tried to stand up but her legs were trembling so much, she collapsed back into her chair.

And then she saw her tape recorder sitting on the desk.

She had forgotten to turn it off.

Now a burst of rage and energy flooded her body. She went to the desk and re-ran the tape and switched it on. It was all there.

Agatha picked up the phone and dialled Mircester police headquarters and explained she had the real murderer. She got put straight through to Wilkes, who listened in astonished silence and then began to rap out questions: When had he left; what car was he driving?

When Agatha replaced the phone, she wondered whether to call John and then decided against it. Although she would never admit it to herself, she viewed his pursuit of Charlotte Bellinge as a rejection of herself. She phoned the vicarage instead, only to learn that Mrs. Bloxby was out. The doorbell went. It couldn't be the police already. Agatha went into the kitchen and slid a knife out of the drawer and approached the door. She peered through the peep-hole in the door and saw, with a flood of relief, the elderly face of Ralph Crinsted under a dripping hat.

"You'll never guess what's happened!" she cried, brandishing the kitchen knife in her excitement.

"Be careful with that knife, Agatha," he said nervously.

"Oh, what? Gosh, I was frightened. The police are on their way."

"May I come in? It's awfully wet."

"Yes, come along."

"I hope I'm not disturbing you; I thought up a few ideas for the old folks' club. You seem to be in the middle of a drama."

Agatha led him into the sitting-room. "I don't know about you, but I would like a large brandy. Care to join me?"

"Why not."

Once the drinks were poured, Agatha got half-way through the story when Bill Wong arrived with another detective.

He asked to hear the tape. Agatha switched it on, wincing at the earlier bit, which included the start of her will, and then all her bragging. But then Binser's dry precise voice describing the murders sounded in the room.

"We'll get him," said Bill. "We have his registration number. He'll be stopped before he reaches London. I think we'd better start ferreting in his background. He was up for a knighthood, you know.

"You'd better come back with us to Mircester, Agatha, and make a full statement."

Agatha was taken over her statement again and again until she was gratefully able to sign it. She then had a long talk with Bill which depressed her. He was doubtful whether the tape alone would be enough to convict Binser.

Poor Miss Partle. Had Binser said something to her during his prison visit that had finally tipped her over the edge? Had he always been respectable?

John Armitage watched her climbing out of a police car that evening. He hurried round to her cottage and listened amazed to the story that Agatha was now heartily tired of telling.

"Did they get Binser?" John asked when she had finished.

"He was stopped on the road to London. He's denying everything. He's got a team of lawyers. Bill says they are digging into his past. He says Binser seems always to have been a pretty ruthless person."

"And you thought he was straightforward and decent."

"I got there in the end," said Agatha crossly. "Get your ring all right?"

"Thank you. As a matter of fact, I'm thinking of moving back to London."

"Not a good time to sell. The house market's in a slump at the moment."

"I'll take what I can get, and," John added with a tinge of malice, "I shall think of you down here busy at work on your old folks' club. So Miss Partle's off the hook?"

"If she ever recovers her sanity, she'll probably be charged with aiding and abetting a murderer and attempting to murder me. I'm glad it's all over. It's up to the police now to prove he did it."

"They've got that taped confession."

"Bill told me after I'd made my statement that he might get away with it. He's saying he only told me a load of rubbish because he thought I was so smug. He's insisting it was a joke at my expense. Also, I don't know if that tape would stand up in court. There was no one in authority here, he wasn't cautioned and he wasn't on oath."

"You should be worried. If he gets away with it, he'll come looking for you."

"No, he won't," said Agatha. "I'm no threat to him. He seemed pretty confident I couldn't find out anything. And if they don't get him this time, then they can't charge him with the same crime twice."

"Well, I can't share your confidence. I'd best be off. I've got enough in the bank to rent somewhere in London until this place is sold."

Agatha wanted to say, "Will you miss me? Did you care

anything for me at all?" But fear of rejection kept her silent.

Instead, she said, "I suppose you'll be seeing a lot of Charlotte Bellinge."

"That silly woman," he said viciously. "No. She turned out to be a terrible bore. I shall be glad to return to all the fun and lights of London. The thought of being buried down here in the winter is an awful prospect. I don't know how you cope with it."

"Some people would think three murders was enough excitement for anyone."

"Anyway. See you around, maybe."

John went back to his cottage and stood looking around. May as well think of packing some things up. He'd be glad to get away. And whoever it was that Agatha was romancing, he wished her the joy of him. *He* didn't care. She meant nothing to him. Infuriating woman. And as a proof of his lack of interest in Agatha Raisin, he kicked the wastebasket clear across the room.

# EPILOGUE

†

DESPITE Agatha's assurances to John that she was not worried that Binser would come looking for her, she felt edgy and nervous.

She tried to call Bill several times only to be told that he was not available, and her heart sank. She really should have apologized to him about her remarks about Alice.

So when she opened the door to him a week after Binser had been arrested, she flew at him, crying, "Oh, Bill, I'm so sorry about those dreadful things I said about Alice."

"That's all right," he said. "Let's go in. I've some good news for you. Never mind about coffee," he said, walking with her into the kitchen to a glad welcome from the cats, "I want to tell you right away."

"What?"

"We've got Binser all sewn up."

"How? What happened?"

"Well, I phoned the top psychiatrist at that psychiatric prison she's in and asked how Miss Partle was getting on. He said he was just drafting a report. He said he was rapidly coming to the conclusion that she was faking madness. Maybe she was tired of keeping up the act, but he said twice he had surprised her reading a book with all the appearance of intelligent enjoyment. I talked to my superiors and arranged an interview. She sat drooling in front of me, all blank-eyed. I told her that Binser had confessed. I didn't tell her he might get away with it.

"She looked at me, startled, and then she began to cry. She switched the mad act right off. She said when he had visited her in prison, she had asked him whether he had told his wife yet that they were going to get married. He said, not yet. He would wait until she was free and then they would run off together. It was that, she said, that suddenly made her realize he was lying, for she knew he would never leave his work. He relished his position and he relished power. But she did not know what to do. She still loved him, however, still hoped. She said she had sunk so low that all she wanted to do was live in the hope of seeing him again. He told her if she faked madness, then she wouldn't stand trial.

"I was wondering how to get some actual proof of his culpability out of her, so I said there was no death penalty and she could wait for him, for the charge of conspiracy to murder plus attempted murder would carry less of a sentence. She said she would not have killed you. She had phoned him and he had said to frighten you as much as possible while he worked out what to do. She said she wouldn't actually have hit you with that hammer."

"So how did you get the goods on Binser out of her?" asked Agatha.

"I told her that Binser had told you that he had never loved her and she was easy to use, that he had no intention of ever leaving his wife. She started to cry again, and after a bit she became very angry. Miss Partle said that he had written a confession to the murders so that after his death, she would be exonerated. Why she fell for that one, I do not know, as he could have outlived her. I asked where the confession was. She said they had various subsidiary companies, and in the safe of an office in Docklands, we would find a confession.

"Once started, it seemed she could not stop. She told me about insider trading deals, intimidation of companies he wished to take over, the lot. I couldn't believe my luck. I phoned Wilkes, who said he would be down hotfoot with two detectives and a tape recorder. I was terrified while I waited that she would regret the whole thing and slip back into her pretended madness. We raided the safe of a company called Hyten Electronics, and there was the confession along with a set of account books he certainly would not want the income-tax people to see. So he's been charged."

"What a relief," said Agatha. "I told John I was sure he wouldn't come looking for me, but I'd begun to jump at every sound."

"Where is John? There's a FOR SALE sign outside his cottage."

"He's going to rent a flat in London. He's already sent off most of his stuff."

"That's quick work."

"Oh, it's easy to rent a flat in London if you've got the money."

"So no engagement?"

"No, there wasn't enough there. I gave him back his ring."

"Did that upset you?" Bill looked at her shrewdly.

"Not very much. He was a bore," said Agatha, unconsciously echoing John's remark about Charlotte Bellinge. "And I hope everything is all right with you and Alice?"

"Well, no, it isn't."

"I'm sorry, Bill. It was that dreadful wine. I should never have let her have any."

"I'd got over that. People say things when they are drunk they don't really mean. She was rude to Mother."

Agatha felt a pang of sympathy for Alice.

"What did she say?"

"Well, Mother always does jump the gun a bit. She was saying how Alice and me could save money after we were married by moving in with them—Mum and Dad, that is. Alice said to her, 'Don't be ridiculous. I've already picked out a nice bungalow for us.' I pointed out it was the first I'd heard of it. Alice said, 'I couldn't live here. They'd drive me mad.'

"I got very angry but I still thought it was maybe the wrong time of the month or something. Alice insisted we drive out of Mircester on the other side of the ring road, where she said this bungalow was. It was quite large. An estate agent was showing a couple round. I asked how much it was selling for and he said one hundred and eighty thousand. I pointed out to Alice I could never afford that. My pay isn't great, you know. She asked why I hadn't saved anything, living at home. I said I paid Mum and Dad for my keep. She went absolutely ballistic and called me all kinds of fool. So I told her I never wanted to see her again."

"Don't you want to live on your own?" asked Agatha curiously. "There's police accommodation in Mircester, isn't there? Get your independence."

"I have my independence," said Bill, puzzled. "All my meals are prepared for me and I have my own room at home."

Agatha decided to drop the subject. "I feel a fool the way

I went on," she said. "I was completely taken in by Binser."

"He's the fool," said Bill. "He was very lucky no one ever saw him. Mrs. Bloxby saw you leaving Tristan's at midnight. Pity she didn't look out of the window later on in the night. Miss Jellop's neighbours happened to be away or busy. Peggy Slither often played loud music and her neighbours aren't all that close to her. Maybe it takes an amateur to find an amateur."

"Except I got the wrong amateur. Did Binser say what he planned to do with me? I mean, I had told John I was going to see Miss Partle."

"He's already accused of enough, so he sticks to the story that he had told Miss Partle to frighten you so that you would drop the whole thing."

"I can't see her believing that."

"She was so much in love with him and already in such a state of panic that she didn't think clearly."

"I never saw a less frightened woman."

"Maybe he planned to dump your body somewhere and then arrange things so that it would look as if you had left the country. I don't know. I think you should take things easy from now on, Agatha."

"I plan to."

In the weeks leading up to Christmas, Agatha threw herself into preparations for the old folks' club. She raised money by deciding after all to hold an auction and then held several bingo evenings in the school hall, much to the distress of the vicar, who felt it was encouraging gambling.

The opening party on Christmas Eve was a great success. The ladies' society organized a roster of drivers to take the infirm elderly to the club.

In the new year, Ralph Crinsted started his chess classes.

Agatha felt mildly guilty that she had done nothing about taking further lessons from him, although he seemed to have a good few willing pupils.

It was the end of January before she realized that the FOR SALE sign outside John's cottage had gone.

Agatha hurried along to the vicarage. "Who's my new neighbour?" she asked Mrs. Bloxby.

"I believe it is a certain Mr. Paul Chatterton, some sort of computer expert."

"Oh, some computer nerd. Anyway, I'm not interested in men anymore. I thought John might have called at least once."

"I wouldn't worry about him. I think he was a bit of a lightweight."

Agatha looked at her in surprise. It was highly unusual for the vicar's wife to say anything critical about anyone.

Mrs. Bloxby coloured. "I do not like the way he treated you. I do wish you would find someone suitable."

"I tell you, I've given up. There aren't any suitable men when you get to my age, anyway."

"God will provide," said Mrs. Bloxby sententiously.

Agatha grinned as a vision of a handsome bachelor, gift-wrapped, and descending from heaven, entered her mind.

When she walked back to her cottage, she saw there was a removal van outside. Overseeing the unloading of it was what was obviously the new tenant. He was middle-aged but tall and fit-looking. He had a shock of white hair and a thin, clever face and sparkling black eyes.

Agatha hurried indoors. She picked up the phone and made an appointment with the hairdresser and then the beautician.

Not that she was interested in men anymore.

Still, it didn't do to let oneself go.